I0684371

EliteRoyalties LLC Publications

"WAIT'N FOR THE SUN TO RISE"

A NOVEL BY

Geoffrey McClanahan

Published by Elite Royalties LLC Publications

All rights reserved. Without limiting the rights under copyright reserved above. No part of this book may be reproduced, stored in or introduced into a retrieval system, or transmitted, in any form, or by any means (electronic, mechanical, photocopying, recording, or otherwise), without prior written consent from both the author, and publisher Elite Royalties LLC Publications, except brief quotes used in reviews.

PUBLISHER'S NOTE:

This book is a work of fiction. Names, Characters, Places, and incidents either are products of the author's imagination or are used fictitiously. Any resemblance to actual events or locales or persons, living or dead, is pure and entirely coincidental.

Copyright © 2011 by Geoffrey McClanahan
All Rights Reserved, including the right of reproduction in whole or in part of any form.
ISBN 978 - 0 - 9835896 - 1 — 7

Author: Geoffrey McClanahan
Cover Design: Brand Concepts Creative Media
Interior Format: Write On Promotion

ACKNOWLEDGMENTS

I first give God praise for giving me the breath I breathe and the talent for which he has chosen to bless me with. I give special thanks to: my mother, Gloria McClanahan, who consistently pushed me to recognize my untapped talents and to turn negative situations into positive pathways for success. Thank you for being a supportive friend, my "third eye", and a mentor. Most importantly I give special thanks to My Female Cousin "Marshyne Merritt", who's death and murder at such a young age because of a domestic, violent relationship in 2005, inspired me to right this book. May you look down and be proud! We love you and miss you dearly. To any women or young female who feels like they can't get out.

Speak up!

Stand up for yourself!

Don't be afraid!

Don't let domestic violence keep you down.

Geoffrey McClanahan

Authors Note:

Definition of Violence

Violence is the threatened (or) actual use of physical force (or) power against another person, against oneself, or against a group (or) community that either results in, or has a high likelihood of resulting in injury, death or depreciation.

Domestic violence is a growing problem across the United States. Statistics reveal that in almost one-third of all willful homicides, the victim was killed by a spouse, parent or child.

"WAIT'N FOR THE SUN TO RISE"

CHAPTER I

"THE NIGHT BEFORE"

I woke up in a tremor with my head instinctively jolting backward. As if a bug skittered across my face. I then realized it was a hand. A woman's hand. I thought to myself, "Oh shit, I did it again." I had brought home some promiscuous chick who must have had a low level of self-esteem. If she was sleeping with a strange man she just met at a night club. Maybe she was just like me. Taking on a quick fuck to hide in the realities of a pathetic lifestyle based on emotionless sex; Never ever wanting to explore the possibilities of a commitment.

I couldn't see her face, because her head was wedged between two throw pillows I had purchased at a two-for-one sale at Macy's on 34th Street the weekend before. Fuck the fact: I don't even know this woman from a whole in the wall. I was more concerned if this chick's hair was real. I could never get used to all that weave and hair tracks that some women find attractive. Maybe I'm overreacting a little bit. But getting all those strains of leftover hair off my bed gets to be a bit annoying at times. Also, leaving all that evidence behind for the next chick to find is not in a player's best interest. Slowly brushing my hand over her scalp, I was happy to feel that the roots were all hers. I let out a soft sigh of relief. I smiled and then ran my hand down my six pack to my pubic hairs and grabbed myself.

That's right: I'm an arrogant and conceited fuck when it comes to sex. The woman in my bed was out cold. so I guess it was safe to say, I've rocked that pussy to sleep. The vision of last night popped in my head like I'd just pressed the rewind button on my Toshiba DVD entertainment system. The thought of her being unattractive was erased immediately. Because she was a serious dime piece. I had remembered thinking for a split second while in the club, Damn this chick was fine when I first caught a glimpse of her face.

1:10am at Club Lotos in Soho, I had turned to my boy Kurt after walking around the club for a few minutes while sipping on my drink and asked.

"Yo – is that that actress Lucy Liu over there at the bar?"

Even he did a double take.

"Yo, that chick is fine as fuck. You should go for it playboy." Kurt said with a big ass smile on his face.

I gave him the normal hood handshake. But feeling a little annoyed at the same time. I've grown tired of how black men conduct themselves in public places. I gave him the lip twisted up, head nod, homeboy response. That night I just felt like being on some mature shit for once.

The bass was loud, and the club was packed with tits and ass. Young wannabe gangsters and a small group of Wall Street buppies trying to pretend that they were a part of the street life. I had a few drinks before even entering the club. So I was already on that arrogant bullshit from jump street. Everything, and everyone became a target for me to throw darts at. Trying to avoid my own insecurities that I hidden very well deep inside. Me Snapping out of that thought, I noticed that Kurt had already walked off. I watched him blend into the crowd. He was on the crowded dance floor grinding with a Sister, who if I might say so myself, had what men called a serious fatty.

I smiled as I watched her big apple bottom butt bounce to the song blaring out of the speakers. R&B singer "Usher's" club banger "Caught Up." I said to myself, what the hell, I came out to have fun. So stop acting like a little bitch. I then remembered that fine woman in the corner I noticed when I walked in.

I grabbed my designer button-up shirt, straightened it out, ran my fingers over the brim of my $120 fedora hat, and started to walk towards her. The closer I got, I could see that two brothers were trying to spit game. The expression on her face let me know that she was not going for the average bullshit whispered in her ear. This pleased me in a way, because she displayed a certain sense of maturity that I liked. I also noticed how she gave the brothers a kind smile as she, in fact, shot them down. That was the true reality of the situation. I slowed my pace gathering my thoughts on how to approach her without giving her the same tired and corny lines that she had probably already heard within the first half hour of being there. The closer I got, I could see all the beautiful splendor that defined every part of her face.

"What the fuck?" spilled out of my mouth quicker than the thought itself. I could not believe how fine this woman was. She surely had to have strayed away from her tribe off of some secluded island from Japan. Or somewhere out of fine ass land. Even those blue and red lights that spin on and off the crowd could not counteract the intensity of her complexion that seemed to serve as a shield reflecting any invading colors other than her own skin tone.

Then it happened! She turned her head to the left and there I was, like a 5-year-old in a Toys R Us, mesmerized by the toys displayed on shelves labeled free for the taking. My mouth wide open, and my eyes popped out of my head. I was caught. Straight with no chaser.

"Can't turn back now," I said to myself closing my mouth. I thought, "Fuck that, I can't be a punk now. I'm just gonna step to mine's and handle my business." I was already twisted on the Hennessy & coke that Kurt and I had drank when we entered the club. But that's exactly what I did. Step to my business.

I walked straight up to her, pulled the seat up next to hers and sat down. No doubt, I did it in a way to demonstrate that I had some class. I said, "Excuse me" to the person sitting next to her chair. The young lady was in deep conversation with a brother that looked cooler than Denzel Washington in that movie "Training Day." I also gave him the hood nod and head up for being patient as I squeezed myself between her and the young lady I was pursuing that night. He gave me the same reply letting me know that he had some self-confidence as well. We were both obviously aware of the outcome of drama in nightclubs. I noticed him scanning my face checking out the war scars. If he was thinking they were probably from some street beef. If that was the case in fact, then he was correct for thinking so. I also noticed that his bottom lip had been stitched also. It was not a fresh scar, and was probably from the same scenario. An old-school street beef. So we played it cool. Like two ice cubes floating in water – smooth.

Crazy as it sounds, I wasn't even the first one to start up the conversation. As I was turning my head to finally get the words out barely not knowing what I was going to say, or how I planned to come at this fine woman, she cut my words short with,

"I like that. I like that a lot in a man."

The expression on her face wasn't what I expected at all. I expected a reaction like, "here we go with some flyboy, pretty boy, pushing up all in my face." That was not her response, not the response at all. Instead, the expression on her face softened. It gave me the impression that I had saved her from a horrible and scary nightmare. It seemed as though she was feeling safe and happy that I had finally showed up to hold her close and tell her everything was going to be okay. I'm here now and your safe. She had one leg crossed over the other revealing her smooth legs through the slit in her summer dress. I held myself back from touching her leg. Wanting to find out how soft those legs really were. Instead, I replied,

"Thank you for the compliment."

"Your welcome." she smiled.

"I like that in a woman." I shot back at her.

She responded with a loud laugh.

"Like what in a woman?"

"I like the fact that you recognize a real gentleman when you see one."

We continued to talk about who we were, and what our occupations were. We got so caught up in enjoying each other's stories, that we didn't even exchange names in all that time talking. I finally asked her what her name was and where did she get her exotic features.

"My name is Mayee."

"Mayee? What is that?" I asked.

"That's Japanese."

"WOW!" I said dragging the vowel out in a mocking tone like I had never seen an African-American mixed with Asian features before.

At first I thought I had offended her because her expression quickly shifted after I had given her my reply. But then she smiled. And by the way she smiled, I could see that she was seriously buzzed. She leaned forward almost falling completely off of her seat. I reacted reflectively and just as I caught her, my hand landed dead center on her breast, and the other one under her armpit. She gave me a strange look at first, but then she asked me in a sexually seductive whisper if she could go to my place that night.

Now when I would ask a pretty young lady if I could go to her place for the night, I wouldn't say it out loud, but my true thoughts were - "I just don't want to be alone tonight." It was never about the sex. Just my way of not having to deal with personal or emotional issues. Sex was simply the activity I used to block it out for that moment.

The rest of that night seemed to continue in a direction that gave me a feeling that there was more to this woman than just a one night stand. Tonight might not be a one-and-done situation for me.

I was now curious as to what she was hiding? What she was trying to escape from? If there was a who she was running from?

I said to myself "Fuck it" and told her I had to find my friend Kurt to let him know I was leaving for the night. Then I thought about how many times his selfish ass had left me sitting around like a fucking owl on a tree branch waiting for him to return and say lets go.

So I quickly scanned the dance floor and spotted him all up in some women's face. I figured that he was going to probably get himself some ass anyway and bounce on me again. So he will be just fine. I grabbed her hand and headed for the exit.

My truck was parked in one of those 24 hour garages on Houston Street. So we had time to enjoy a little air on the way. She didn't say much. I guess she was still feeling a bit tipsy. Her arms were crossed, and her eyes had a droopy kind of look to them. She noticed me checking her out through the corner of my eye. Then she just smiled and giggled.

"What's so funny?" I asked as I smiled too.

"I am fucking flying right now."

She said rolling her eyes and sucking her teeth.

She was seriously twisted when she made the comment.

I placed my arm around her waist and put my hand on her hip. Kinda closer to her left ass cheek. I pulled her inward towards me. Walking in lower Manhattan late at night always gave me a content feeling inside. It's something about the lights. The quietness. She leaned her head on my shoulder as we strolled into the garage. I paid the gateman. "Habeeb" is what I called him. He was from Pakistan. Us People from New York always have a nickname for all foreigners that come to New York for whatever reason. Habeeb handed me my keys and smiled.

He leaned forward and whispered in my ear.

"Hey, she is a beautiful one my friend." He said that there was something special about her and that she was a keeper.

His accent always made me laugh no matter what he was saying. She looked at him with one eyebrow up and her lips twisted. I hurried him along so she wouldn't feel in any way disrespected or insulted by his comment. We were real silent all the way to my truck.

"Before I open the door, I just want you to know that there is no pressure on my end. If you feel like you want to change your mind, please say so now." I asked in a calm manner.

She said no. And that she was fine. So with that being said, I drove my truck like I had no disregard for the speed limit whipping in and out of traffic and running almost every red light to my place where we wounded up having hot heavy sex until we passed out in each other's arms. Later, I was awoken by her hand pasted to my face.

CHAPTER II

"Now I Know"

I softly removed Mayee's hand from my face placing her arm by her side. She opened her eyes slowly looking right into my mines.

"What are you doing?"

"I'm going to make us some breakfast."

"Make us some breakfast?"

"Yeah," I smiled.

"I wish my fiancé was like you."

I paused for a few seconds with this silly look on my face. For the first time, in a long time, I had a woman in my bed who was honest from the door. From the way she said it, it almost seemed like we had known each other for a while. There was no way I was going to even go there on some bullshit. I had to think fast. And think of a response.

"Think quick," I said to myself. Search for the right comeback. Don't panic man, be cool. Remember, like an ice cube in a glass of water...smooth." I let my legs rest over the edge of my bed as I reached for my underwear.

"Kevin! Kevin! Kevin?"

"Oh shit! I'm sorry Mayee."

She had called me three times before I had snapped out of my thoughts.

"Was I wrong for saying I had a fiancé?"

"No! Hell no! You see that's the problem with people today. We are never honest and straight to the point. There's always a game being played. Or lying about the truth. I respect the truth."

"And what's the truth to you?"

She asked putting her arm around my waist, letting her hand rest on my pubic hairs as she played with them waiting for an answer.

"The truth is you're not happy with your decision."

"What decision?"

"The decision to stay in that relationship that has you running."

"What makes you think I'm running?"

She took the top sheet and wrapped herself in it covering her breasts. Then she sat straight up while leaning her back against the headboard. She squinted her eyes and waited for more.

I stood up to put my underwear on. Then I turned to her running my fingers through her long and silky hair brushing the loose hairs from off the front of her face.

"Well Mayee. I believe relationships are about choices and decisions. You choose to accept the things you like or dislike in someone, and then you decide if you are willing to sacrifice what makes you comfortable or uncomfortable to deal with in that relationship."

After a brief pause, I walked away leaving her sitting on the bed. I like to do shit like that. Watching a woman's face when I say some intellectual, thought-provoking shit.

While making my way into my kitchen, I was hoping she was right behind me. Hoping she wanted to continue on with the topic conversation. I reached into the fridge grabbing eggs and butter off of the top shelf. I also grabbed some tomatoes, onions, ham and cheese. I was going to make my infamous Spanish omelet that my mother and sister had only had the honors of enjoying on a Sunday morning before heading of to church. I started to think about how long it's been since I had seen them both. My mother and sister. She walked into the kitchen with the sheet still wrapped around her. This time her hair was in a ponytail, and her face was still wet from a quick rinse.

"You think you're slick pretty boy."

"How's that little Jade?"

"You think because you say some intelligent shit, I was going to curl up inside."

"I don't want you to curl up at all."

"So, what do you want?"

"What do I want?"

I continued to crack the eggshells against the bowl using the time to think of what to say. Normally I would have a quick comeback line. But because she was so open and cut to the chase with her attitude, I wanted to be real with her, and real with myself. Everything leading up to this point had been pure and honest between us. I did not want to spoil the energy in the atmosphere. I sensed we had a lot to learn from each other. So I was going to answer the question honestly.

"I want you to take your time and see if you want to continue this."

"Continue seeing you? or fucking you?"

"Damn Girl, you just are full of surprises!"

I bit my bottom lip in a sensual playful way as I reached for her soft and sexy body. I grabbed her by her shoulders and pressed her against the counter with strength.

I put my hand under the sheet forcing my fingers up, and inside her pussy slowly. She started breathing heavy in short. And then long breaths. Then she let the sheet drop to the floor wrapping around her ankles. Looking at her perfect body only made me hornier. My dick was rubbing against her thigh wanting to penetrate that wet and creamy pussy. With both hands, I spun her around with her ass upward, and her stomach resting over the kitchen counter. I began to spread her legs with my feet. With my dick in my hand, I guided it in between her ass cheeks. I leaned forward slowly so it could go in softly. Then I was inside her slowly pumping away...pumping with every intent to please. I started to go harder and deeper forcefully. I put one hand on her ass cheek, and the other one on her head. I started to pull her hair getting real excited. I closed my eyes feeling the desires of pleasure and enjoyment. She whispered, "Stop" Then again, "Stop" pushing softly against my waist. Before I could slow down the tempo, she let out a loud scream. "Stop it I said Goddamn it! Get the fuck off of me!"

She pushed my body off of hers with sudden force, and then swung at my face. In the midst of her sudden outburst, she kicked me in the balls at the same time. Dropping towards the floor, on my way down, I could see that her eyes were closed. As if she was not really fighting me but, a ghost? I was already on the floor trying to catch a wind, but she continued to swing in mid-air with her eyes still closed beginning to water up. Then she stopped suddenly. Both her arms frozen in midair. Her eyes opened up with tears poring down her face. Her mouth was wide open with surprise.

The room filled with silence. Except for the frying pan on the stove that her hand had hit which began making a noise like a penny spinning on a counter top. When it finally fell crashing to the floor, we both looked at it on the floor. Then we made eye contact.

The silence continued for 15-20 seconds. She took a deep breath and spoke.

"Oh my God! Oh my God! I'm so so sorry Kevin."

I sat there completely puzzled. I was in total shock. In my head I was saying over and over, that this bitch has some serious fucking issues. I didn't want to say that out loud, so I just questioned.

"What the fuck was that?"

I started to get up covering my balls. She was not going to get another shot at the family jewels. I let her know that I was not going to make her anymore angrier than she already was. If that's what it was, anger.

She walked towards me helping me to regain my balance. She kept on saying softly in my ear.

"I'm so sorry. I'm so sorry, Kevin."

She pushed me against the fridge softly and grabbed a cloth to wipe the blood off my bottom lip. She washed my face as we stood there in silence. When she was finished, she put both her hands on my chest leaning her forehead in the center.

"I think it's time for me to go. Are you okay Kevin?"

"I don't know what I am Mayee, but we can talk about it if you want."

"No, I think I've embarrassed myself enough."

I placed my hand on the side of her face stroking it gently. It wasn't hard to tell at that point what was going on. Mayee had man issues. I knew someone was abusive to her mentally and physically. I did not want to press her at that point. I had to make a choice and a decision now. Do I want to continue that kind of relationship or not? She decided to take shower and wind down a bit. I sat my black ass on the couch to process what just happened. Next to my right thigh was her purse and a grey T-Mobile sidekick phone where she had placed them both when she first came into my apartment and sat down. I let out a soft sigh and tried to relax. And then suddenly, the sound of 50Cents' "In the club" came to tune from her sidekick. I was feeling that 50Cent joint, so I picked it up and put it to my ear. My finger must have hit the flip open, revealing the screen for my eyes to see. I was trying to be cool and not be the nosy one, but I couldn't contain my curiosity. The screen flashed "You've got E-mail." I knew it would be wrong to sneak a peak, but she made me feel a need to know what she did and who she really was. So I pressed enter. The message displayed. I started to read it and just as I had predicted,

"Where the fuck are you Mayee? I called Theresa's house to see if you were over at her place and she told me, 'Don't be calling her house looking for you.' Fuck that bitch. Come home, baby. I was a little upset...you know I have to run the law firm when he goes on vacation. You know the fucking drill...Bring your ass home!"

I heard the shower water shut off. So I closed the sidekick and put it back down. I gritted my teeth with disgust. I now knew it was that bitch ass fiancé of hers. It's a fucking joke to these kind of men. You know the type, insecure ass niggaz. I don't like to call my black people Niggaz, but some of them just fit that stereo typed description.

Mayee came out in a rush grabbing her summer dress, pulling it over her head then letting it drop to her knees. She then slipped her feet into a pair of stiletto heels. Classy ones. Prada or Gucci, I couldn't tell. But they were real nice and expensive. She grabbed her sidekick phone and opened it to see if she had any messages. She sucked her teeth and closed the phone. She grabbed my face and kissed me on my lips, slow and soft. She put her hands on her hips, and stared at me for a few seconds.

"So where do we go from here Kevin?"

"How about you just take my number and call me any time you need to see me." I replied back.

"I'm not crazy, Kevin."

"I know who he is, Mayee." I said calmly.

"I don't know what to do Kevin. What do I do?"

We both looked at each other. I was stuck between a rock and a hard place. I knew where all of this could go. I wasn't ready for this type of shit.

"I don't know either, Mayee. I just don't know at this point myself, but I really want to..."

She smiled and turned around and went straight for the door. She opened it and walked right out without even turning back to say goodbye. I put my face in both of my palms and sat there in silence. I gathered my thoughts for a few seconds, and went back into the kitchen to clean up that mess. As I was cleaning, everything replayed over and over again in my head. I finished up quickly and laid back down in my bed to take a quick nap. While staring up at the ceiling I dozed off.

Chapter III

"Motherly Advice"

Three weeks have gone by since I've spoken to anyone besides Kurt. My work load has gotten real demanding in the past few days. Some people have no idea how much work needs to be done in the culinary field. My job title is an Assistant Head Chef. I do most of the cooking all the time, because the Head Chef of most kitchens has more paperwork to do than cooking. Which consists of food inventory, changing menus, setting up corporate banquets and making sure that they have enough staff to cover all of the corporate events. Most of the workers are from the best culinary temp agencies in the NYC Midtown district. I also began my cooking career by working through the temp agencies before I advanced to the position I have now. I currently work at the Financial Center off of the West Side Highway across from Ground Zero 9/11 disaster. The corporate kitchen is located in the Merrill Lynch building. That's where I can be found doing what I enjoy: prepping food, making all kinds of famous and tasty sauces from scratch, for fancy dishes from Italian and French recipes.

It was Friday afternoon, and my 6:00 a.m. - 2:00 p.m. shift was coming to an end. Kathy was one of the most outspoken employees that worked by my side most of the day. She was a Hispanic woman with long red hair that drops down to the arch in her back. She kept it up in a ponytail during work hours, because that was a health code rule. She was 37 years old, and 4 years my senior. She was a serious flirt when it came down to me. When we were not in plain sight, we would happily exchange body brush-ups and a few ass grabs throughout the day. Today she hit me with some new shit out of the blue. On our way out from the days work into the hallway while walking alone to the elevator, she got at me hard body.

She placed her hand on my shoulder and she whispered in my ear.

"Cuando vamos a chingar?"

"What?"

"Cuando vamos a chingar?"

"That shit sounds real sexy Kathy."

"You wanna know what I asked?"

"Hell yeah."

"I asked you, when are we going to fuck."

I burst out in laughter. Then I grabbed her pulling her close to me. I told her, if she kept on saying shit like that, she would wind up pissing on parts of her uterus fucking around with me. I teased her about her age as I palmed her fat ass. Before she could say anything back, other employees leaving for the day began to crowd the hallway. So we changed the subject. On the elevator, I told her I was on my way to catch up with my mother before she went to lunch. My mother also worked around Ground Zero a few blocks away. She kissed me on my cheek and told me to enjoy my weekend.

I called my mother's cell phone, because she worked at a very elite law firm. She had a conspiratorial attitude when it came to her job. She's always said that "Big Brother" was always watching. I love that about my mother. She always has jokes. We have a very open relationship compared to your average single black parent family. She had always taught me and my siblings to be honest about anything we were going through. She would never take sides, or judge us in anyway. I also realized that I hadn't been by to see her on the last three weekends either. Our weekends together were becoming redundant. The same shit. Talking about our jobs and criticizing everyone but ourselves. The topic about Mayee was sure to spice things up. I thought for a second. Damn! I was late in calling her before she had left.

"Hello, Gigi speaking."

"Hey Lady."

"Oh my God, I was just thinking about your ass kid."

"What's good with you Mom?"

"You know I hate talking in my office."

"So get up off your ass and come down for lunch. I got some juicy shit to talk about."

"OH DAMN! Just when I had some down time from dealing with your sister's shit."

"For real Mom, I think you might want to hear this."

"Okay, I'm on my way down."

My mother was very Pro-Black. Even more so when it came to domestic violence. She gets real deep when it comes to women. She believes in helping all women. But she definitely goes in hard when it comes down to Black Women. She does pro bono work for women of abuse in her spare time.

She even invites Black women from the shelters for, abused women, over once a month for a home-cooked dinner in order to give them some down time.

For a quick minute past images in my head began to replay my early years being a toddler. I remembered my father beating on my mother under the influence of alcohol and drugs. My mother had three brothers. So that shit lasted a short time. He had never kept in contact with me and brother or sister, so I grew up not knowing him at all. Back then was nothing like the "Bill Cosby show" at all.

I loved going to lunch with my mother. Because all the sexy and classy sisters that worked in her building would crowd the lobby during the midtown lunch hours. I use to flirt like crazy to see how many numbers I could get while waiting for her. Today was different. I had Mayee on my mind heavy. I needed some adult shit to go down today. I watched my mother get off the elevator and make her way through the crowd. My mother was not remotely old fashioned. She always dressed to impress in the best designer outfits. Prada, Dolce Gabana, Ann Taylor, Gucci, -- and kept her hair tight. She gave me a kiss on my cheek and handed me her purse. She always had something to look for in her purse. Unbelievable!

"What's popping' homes?" she said giggling. "What's good my snizzle?" which was slang for son. She always tried to use street slang in a joking manner to get a laugh out of me.

We had a good laugh together, and headed onto the streets to have lunch. We would go to a nice little restaurant café around Broadway or Wall Street, one of those streets. It was her little getaway. We entered the restaurant, placed our orders, received our meals and found a secluded corner table to chat. She stopped with the jokes to get serious.

"So, what's wrong son?"

"I met someone a couple of weeks ago."

"And what's the problem now?"

"She's in an abusive relationship."

"And what part do you play in it?"

"Mom!" I shouted.

"I'm asking are you trying to save her?"

"I don't know."

"You do know son. You know exactly what your intentions are from the time that you found out."

"Why do you do that shit Mom?" I asked.

"Don't even come at me with that. You called me up searching for the fucking oracle, like this is 'The Matrix.'"

"Mom chill! I don't want this to turn into some unnecessary argument. I just don't know what to do at this point."

"Has she told you she was being abused?"

"No, not exactly," I said in a low tone.

"Listen son, I know how you felt about me and your father. But some things have to be resolved between that woman and the man she's with. Two things are going to happen: One, you are going to put yourself in harm's way. You have no idea how this man operates. Two, you're going to give that poor girl false hope that she is being rescued from her situation. The situation is not in her way. She's in her own way. She has to face that demon that chases her. You can take her to fucking Japan, and she would still fear that man. So please baby, be careful in making that move."

She then quoted a statement from the movie "The Matrix" trying to be funny again:

"You've already made the choice Neo! Now you have to understand the choice Neo!"

"Mom, you're fucking crazy."

We laughed and continued to talk about my younger sister Kiki. Keisha was her name. But nicknames are common amongst us black folk. She told me that Kiki was upset, because I wasn't spending anytime with her and my niece like I used to. She would complain about my friends and the women I chose to spend most of my weekends with. She was truly an over-exaggerator. I had spent more time driving all over the upstate area in shopping malls, buying shit for her, than I did for myself. But, I love every minute of it. She is my heart and soul. And she knows that, all she has to do is cry and whine over the phone and I'm there to respond to her every request.

I walked my mother back to her building and offered her some money. But she always turned it down.

"Nigga please! Keep your small chump change."

She said with a smile on her face. I mean, I made some good cash, but she was at a higher financial level than I could ever be at that point in my own career. She gave me a kiss goodbye, and told me to call her about Mayee if I was going to see her again.

"Sure Mom, anything you say," I replied back while walking away.

Halfway to my truck my cell phone rang. The number displayed "Private Caller". I knew it was

Kurt because he was always avoiding women calling his number. I answered my phone quickly.

"What the fuck is up my Nigga?"

"What the fuck is up Punk Ass. Yo, you bounced on me that night, faggot. What's good for tonight?"

"Yo, Kurt, you be on some bullshit."

"I'm just fucking around Kevin."

"Yeah, I know my dude. Listen man, meet me at the crib in two hours okay?"

"Yeah, no doubt,"

Kurt said laughing. We hung up at the same time and I headed home.

CHAPTER IV

"WE STILL LOVE THE HOOD"

No matter how many times me and Kurt got together we always had to let it be known that, just because you're not playing the game, doesn't mean that the games still not in you. Here we are both in our early 30's still having the need to constantly floss. Yes, we both have nice apartments and all the added extras that go with the lifestyle. I myself had an obsession for bracelets and watches. I owned seven bracelets and six watches. Not including all the old school name brand watches, such as "Fossils" and "Swatch." Colorful watches from the mid 80s that I kept in an old shoe box in my walk-in closet. Four of the seven bracelets had been gifts from my mother and sister through my years growing into manhood. They were all gold of course. And if you can remember, back in the day, Gucci links was the shit. If your gold chain or bracelet did not weigh 120 grams or more, then what was the use of even buying one. The other three bracelets were all iced the fuck out. I mean, a lot of diamonds. The last one I bought was platinum. And yes that shit broke the piggy bank. But I managed to stay afloat. There was a "Jacob jewelers" watch that I put on my VISA card. That too has some serious Bling-Bling. I put on one of my thick bracelets, a pair of Pelle Pelle jeans and black long-sleeved thermal. With the face of the late great notorious Biggie Smalls printed on the front. I grabbed a pair of black Timberland boots out of the closet to match the shirt. I went into the bathroom so I could give myself a quick hairline edge up. For some strange reason, my gut was on serious alert for drama that night. I could feel those senses tingling. like every time it thunders, plus lightning, but theres no rain?

On my way out of the bathroom my phone rang. "Here we go with the bullshit," I thought.

I picked up the phone and answered,

"What's popping. And who's this?"

It was my sister Kiki on the other end sounding frantic and speaking real fast. I told Kiki to slow the hell down, and be clearer about what the problem was. She took a deep breath and started to tell me about how her boyfriend was drunk and making a big scene in front of the Magic Johnson Movie Theater in Harlem. She told me he had gotten all crazy about her being hugged up under our cousin Chris, who lives a couple of blocks from the theater. She told me that she had tried to explain that Chris was family, but her boyfriend James always had this fucked up attitude about other men touching her. Even family members. I told her to keep that mother fucker right there, and to just go along with his shit until I arrived. I lived on 95th Street between Second and Third Avenues. I knew it would only take five minutes to get to 125th Street from my location.

I put on my Timberlands and reached under my bed for the stash. My uncles taught me that the streets will always be the streets, so it's better to have a gun and not need one, than to need a gun and not have one. So I got two mother fucking guns...Period! I took the 9 mm Beretta out with a full 15-shot clip. I checked the clip and the safety pin just like you see everyone do in the movies. I heard the doorbell ring. I knew it was Kurt. Right on time. I rushed to the door and opened it. The expression on my face spoke volumes when he entered my apartment.

Before I could even get a word out, Kurt started to speak all frantic.

"Yo, I just got a call from baby girl saying this little dude is acting like a fucking fool! Yo, let's go handle this shit!"

Kurt was a little more stuck in his old thug ways than I was. So of course he was carrying a ratchet too. Although I was about handling my business, I was a lot more calm about the situation than Kurt was.

"Kurt, let's just do this smoothly, okay?"

"Yeah, no doubt my nigga!"

Kurt answered with a sinister smile. I knew Kurt well. He was a loose ass dude. He had no problem letting off a few rounds in a nigga. And enjoyed it every time.

We exited my crib and went straight to his car. Kurt was driving a black GS 500 Lexus 2008. Kurt switched cars every other month. I knew that no matter how many legal jobs Kurt had, or no matter how many small businesses he owned, his hands were always in the drug dealing game. A security crutch I suppose. I had given up that part of my life, because it had became a lot more dangerous. And the younger generation played by no rules. Nigga's started to get too damn personal like a fucking woman on her menstrual. These little Nigga's started to come after each other's family members. Mothers, sisters, and even little babies were in the line of fire.

Kurt made it clear that if any real heavy shit was to go down using his car, there would not be any leads to that vehicle. Kurt had a lot of pull in the underworld. He could easily take it to one of his people who owned chop shops and switch it for another within the hour.

Kurt pulled out of the parking space so fast, I thought we were going to hit the other cars parked across the street. He took 95th Street straight up. driving so fast, we shot past every light from Third and Madison Avenues in less than 60 seconds. He then made a right turn onto Lenox Avenue, but slowed up, because he knew that "Po-Po" would probably be on that corner straight on up to 125th Street. We didn't say a word. Not even his CD player was pumping the usual DJ K-Slay mix tape blends. Making the left onto 125th Street, we checked our guns one more time before parking across from the movie theater. I can see my sister and James across the street with a small crowd around them. He had my sister pressed up against a car waving his hand in her face. There were also a lot of the local youngsters around laughing and throwing shit in the game to amp James up. All kinds of cars were parked up and down 125th blaring hip-hop out of their speakers. Police never really came around unless they heard gun fire. And even then it took them 15 to 20 minutes to get to the scene.

Kurt and I jumped out of the car crossing the street and came up behind the crowd. Kurt looked up and down the block for signs of police. He gave me the signal, grabbed his gun, and placed it beside his leg out of sight. I pulled my 9 mm out from my pants and pushed through the crowd. James didn't see me come up behind him. James had his hair in cornrow braids, leaving the ends lying over his shoulders onto his back. I grabbed the ends of his braids spinning him around. I then took the nozzle of my gun and smacked him right across his left cheekbone. Then I hit him again across his nose. Blood shot out of his nose, as he fell to the ground. I grabbed my sister Kiki pushing her behind me in a protective stance. I could see a few people fleeing the scene trying not to get involved making themselves inconspicuous as they walked away. Two of James's friends stood there in shock.

One of them reached for his back. But Kurt had pushed the barrel of his gun onto the back of the kid's head saying to him,

"I don't think you want to do that. Can't you see that's a family beef?"

The young brother froze up and put his hands down to his side. Then he turned around to see who it was that had gotten the drop on him. I didn't know the little fuck head, so I didn't really care. The expression on the boy's face changed real quick when he realized who it was.

"Yo Kurt? That's your...your family? I...I...I swear I didn't know! James is always getting me into some shit. But this time....As a matter of fact? You know what? Fuck that nigga I'm out."

James was lying on his back with blood rolling down both sides of his cheeks. I grabbed his shirt pulling his face closer to mines. I asked him in a whisper,

"What do you think the next best move is?"

With blood coming out of his mouth, he whispered,

"I-I'm going to leave your sister alone."

"I can't hear you James."

"I-I-I'm going to leave your...your sister alone Kevin okay?"

"Much better, James."

I picked him up off the ground and gave him a handkerchief to clean his face and I patted him on his back. I then turned to my sister Kiki and told her that her relationship with him was over. Her arms were crossed over her breasts as she began looking down towards the ground. She was not really feeling what I had said. I grabbed her cheeks and asked her in a stern voice,

"Do you have a problem with that?"

She shook her head and answered "No." Kiki took one last look at James and started to walk across the street towards Kurt's Lexus.

There were two movie theater managers looking on as the whole event took place. Kurt and I knew one of the managers from our hanging out days. His name was Jarvis, but we called him J-Smooth. J-Smooth gave me the hand signal to bounce and get out of there because one of his employees had called the police. The crowd was getting smaller by the seconds. James and his two friends walked off to the car that they were driving. Me and Kurt put both of our guns back into our pants and jogged to the car. Kiki was sitting shotgun playing around with Kurt's CD player. One thing about my sister, she was just like me. Her attitude was, "Hey, it is what it is." Besides, she loved hanging with me and Kurt more than anything. Because she knew she wouldn't have to pay for anything for the rest of that night. I hopped into the back seat behind Kurt's chair. Kurt pulled off with his left hand while Kiki held his right hand.

She turned down the music and said that she loved us very much. Then she giggled and said,

"Now I know you nigga's are going to feed me after beating the shit out of my happy meal."

We all laughed and headed back downtown to 72nd Street and Amsterdam Avenue to eat at the Shark Bar. While waiting for our table, I noticed Kiki starting up again and making herself known to the young gentleman host at the door. Kurt was on his Nextel talking to one of his late night booty calls. Probably setting up for a nightcap quickie after dropping me and Kiki off after we ate. I could hear the cute little hostess behind me trying to get my attention to let us know that our table was ready. I walked up behind Kiki pulling on her ponytail. I told her that it was a long night already, and to forget about the boys for a minute. Then we all sat down and started to scan our menus.

I placed my cell phone on the table and noticed that the time was 12:45 a.m. It was still early and the night was young. Suddenly my phone rang. I looked at the caller ID and saw the name I had been so impatiently waiting to see, speak to, and wanted to touch. Yes, it was Mayee.

I could feel my breath slowly losing its normal rhythm. My heartbeat was regaining its pace. Kiki and Kurt simultaneously pulled their menus down to eye level and stared at me. Kiki raised one eyebrow, as Kurt blurted from behind his menu,

"Nigga, answer your damn phone!"

I grabbed it up quickly and flipped open the door. I was looking real fucking stupid answering the phone with a low-toned voice,

"Hello?"

"Hi." Mayee answered.

"Ummm, hey."

"Ummmm, hi."

Kurt and Kiki burst out laughing loud at the table giving each other a High Five. Kurt said to Kiki,

"Yo, that nigga be fronting hard body!"

Kiki was answering him back saying,

"Word, right."

I put my middle finger up at the both of them and got up from the table for some privacy. I walked to the bathroom and found an empty toilet stall where I could better continue our conversation I private.

"I'm sorry about that Mayee. That was my best friend and my little sister teasing me."

"That's okay, Kevin."

"What's been going on with you?" I asked.

"Oh, I'm just hanging out with my sorority sisters."

"Get the fuck out of here? You belong to a sorority?"

"Yes!" she giggled.

"What sorority?"

"I'm a member of Delta Sigma Theta."

I could hear her friends in the background making the Whoop-Whoop sound as they all laughed in harmony. One of the gals shouted out, "What's up, Kevin?" loud enough for me to hear.

"Who was that?" I asked curiously.

"That would be Patricia."

"She sounds like a fun person to be around."

"Why don't you swing through Queens and hang?"

Without skipping a beat, I answered, "Bet, give me the address."

I took out an old receipt from my wallet and jotted down the directions to her house and the number. I told her it would be a minute, because I had my friend and sister waiting for me to return to the table to dine.

She said, "No problem, just don't be too late sexy."

I hung up the phone and I rushed back to the table. Kiki and Kurt were stuffing their faces with shrimp and Buffalo wings. I asked Kurt to drop Kiki off and I would catch up later with him. Kurt and Kiki knew the drill, so they were not surprised at all. I kissed my sister on the back of her neck, gave Kurt a pound, and made my way to the street for a cab to drive me over the Whitestone Bridge to Queens. It took 20 minutes to find one who was willing to drive that far at that hour of the night. I told him I would give him an extra $20 for his services.

"No problem," the cabbie said and pulled off.

I was on my way to see her. To see the one woman who had me stuck. To see Mayee!

CHAPTER V

"HOW MANY TIMES"

Mayee Kitomaki (Pronounced kee-teo-ma-kee) was her full birth name. Mayee's mother was Japanese and her father was African-American. Sunzu Kitomaki, Mayee's mother, worked for the UN as an interpreter for the Foreign Relations Department for Japan and the United States. Her mother had been disowned for breaking custom and bringing disgrace to her family. By her breaking the pure Japanese bloodline by marrying her Black father, she stayed in the United States in order to continue her education in political science. Because of Mayee's mother's struggle to keep herself from shame, she made sure that Mayee had kept her last name instead of an American last name. Mayee's mother Sunzu had broken the connection between her and her father when Mayee was 3 years old. So Mayee's memories of him were blurred and faded.

Mayee had grown up in Flushing, and then moved to upscale Rosedale Queens in her early teens. Her mother's occupation gave them the luxury of living in a huge home in a quiet community confined by the invisible walls that make New York City the Big Apple. Mayee had graduated with a Biology degree from New York University and now worked at Bellevue Hospital as a Blood Technician. Patricia, Monica, and Theresa had also graduated from NYU along with Mayee. They had all pledged the same sorority, "Delta Sigma Theta" in their first semester at the college.

Patricia and Theresa had lived in the Rosedale area of Queens since birth. Growing up with Mayee since the ages of twelve and thirteen, that made them her best and closest friends. Monica lives in a Co-Op City located in the Bronx. Monica traveled from the Bronx to NYU everyday for her education and had become close with Mayee, Patricia and Theresa when she had pledged Delta Sigma Theta. Theresa also worked at Bellevue Hospital so she and Mayee shared a much stronger relationship than Monica and Patricia.

Theresa was the only one out of the three who knew about Mayee's abusive relationship with Nathan Livingston her fiancé for the past two years. Although he and Mayee had dated five years altogether, Theresa had been through hell with Mayee because of Theresa's many attempts to get in between Nathan's flying fists of the abuse. Theresa, the product of a two-parent home and an only child, felt the need to provide Mayee with a sense of security that she felt she lacked in her single parent home because there was no male figure around to protect her. Plus, in exchange, Mayee gave Theresa the chance to fill the void of not having any brothers or sisters to confide in when times got rough. At Mayee's request, Theresa had promised never to bring her domestic situation to the dinner table.

Patricia was the Tyra Banks of the crew. Monica was rinsing out a hair relaxer that she had put in Patricia's hair 15 minutes earlier as they chilled out at her house. Patricia kept her eyes tightly closed as the water from the kitchen sink splashed all over her neck and head. Even though she had graduated from NYU with a degree in Radiology, she had somehow found her way into the modeling world. She had started working acting as an extra in TV sitcoms like "Girlfriends," "Eve" and

"Half and Half." She was also a client at Faces Models and other famous modeling agencies that provide work for new and old talented and beautiful sisters. She has three summer bikini calendars under her belt. Plus she's been in several hair product commercials as well. To her, her greatest achievement had been having her face displayed on a GAP billboard on 42nd Street alongside four other models. Patricia's body was crazy perfect. Meaning, if you can find anything more perfect, then God must have kept it all to himself. And then there's Halle Berry.

Patricia was wearing a white tank top that came up over her belly button and squeezed both her breasts together tightly showing much cleavage. She had on a pair of grey sweat shorts that also were tight on her perfectly worked-out thighs. She wore no socks or sneakers just bare foot on the kitchen floor. The water flowing off the back of her neck made her nipples perk.

"Damn Pat! What the fuck? I know your ass ain't getting all horny." Monica said jokingly.

"Kiss my ass Monica! Although my Oyster tight pussy hasn't gotten any action since I got back from L.A. two months ago."

"Patricia's pussy's on fire, y'all!"

Monica shouted across the room for Theresa and Mayee to hear while they sat out in the living room having their own private conversation.

"Put some cold water on that shit, Bitch!"

Theresa shouted back while Mayee sat besides her laughing hard as hell.

"Ah ha ha. Ah ha ha," Mayee continued to laugh hard and loud.

"DAMN!"

Monica and Patricia said together causing Patricia to lift her face out of the kitchen sink for a couple of seconds. Theresa turned to Mayee who was leaning back with her mouth wide open,

"Girl, what has gotten into you?"

Silence quickly filled the room. With anticipation everyone waited for Mayee to at least answer the question. Mayee turned her head grabbing her ponytail making an obvious attempt to make them believe she was fixing her hair. If there is one thing a woman knows is when another woman is on some secretive shit.

"Get the fuck out of here! I know?"

Patricia said standing there with water pouring down her face.

"Oh, oh shit...oh shit...oh shit!"

Monica kept saying over and over while jumping up and down in one spot.

"Somebody please tell me this bitch ain't!"

Said Theresa lifting both arms up in the air with her palms facing the ceiling falling off the couch landing on two pillows that were on the floor beside the living room table.

Mayee was sitting in a squatting position on the far corner of the couch. She smiled and placed both hands in a diamond shape form right over her pussy and said,

"She can tell you better than I can."

Patricia does not play when it comes to her hair. But she snatched the towel off Monica's shoulder so fast, she poked herself in the eye rushing to wrap her wet head to keep it from dripping. She wanted to hear the rest of story. Monica had her sneakers on, but slipped on some water as she rushed behind Patricia to get to the couch to hear the juicy news. Theresa sat up and covered her mouth still in shock.

As they all formed a circle getting into a comfortable position to start their meeting, Mayee then said to them,

"You all know the drill. Delta Sigma Theta!"

Patricia, Monica and Theresa each placed their hands one on top of the others and said in harmony, "Delta Sigma Theta!"

When this type of ceremony is performed the person who is speaking tells the story and the other members must not interrupt or make any comments until the person speaking is completely finished. Mayee opened up.

"Take your time, girl," Patricia whispered.

"We got you girl," Patricia whispered again.

"Patricia?" Monica whispered.

"What?"

"Shut the fuck up yo!"

Monica, Theresa and Mayee shouted at the same time. All four of them then started laughing until tears came to their eyes.

"Okay.Okay.Okay," Mayee said seriously.

"His name is Kevin, Kevin Dawson. Not only is he fine, but the brother can cook. He's a chef and he works down by Ground Zero. I was feeling a little down three weeks ago and decided to go to this nightclub and meet one of my co-workers, who asked me to get up with her and have a few drinks, and to unwind for a little bit. She never showed up and I was about to leave because niggas were coming at me with all kinds of corny bullshit. And here comes this fine ass Kevin guy, and Girls it was on!

Then Monica broke the rule by asking Mayee before she could finish,

"Don't you have a fiancé?"

Theresa tightened up her jaw. Because she knew Mayee was finally taking steps towards leaving Nathan. Theresa cut her eyes at Monica and sucked her teeth really loud. Patricia just sat there with the same facial expression from when the question had been asked.

"Anyways..." Mayee said.

"We went back to his place for the night. I guess we did enough talking in the club and in his truck, because we went straight at it from the door. I put my shit down on his couch and he carried me to his bed. When we finally got our clothes all off...Girls, this brother had a perfect dick. Not small at all, but not big either. And I'm not the one for giving head, but I had to suck that shit. The shit he was saying was driving me crazy. He kept saying shit like, 'you are so beautiful,' and that if he could just look at me for a few minutes before he ate my pussy. And he kept running his hands through my hair. And he kept rubbing my face staring in my eyes. Staring at my breasts. Looking me up and down from head to toe. Then he laid me down ever so damned softly and spread my legs gently."

Mayee's eyes started to tear up along with Patricia's as she was holding her hand. Then she continued.

"Then he took his time putting his dick inside me. Slowly, like if he cared about not hurting me, or making me feel uncomfortable. I swear to God, I came before he ever put it in. This brother kept telling me how beautiful I was with every pump. In and out. 'You are so fine. You are a goddess.' It's like he was soothing my soul with every word. Every breath of his emotions. Damn, I haven't felt that in years."

Mayee couldn't hold it anymore. She burst into tears covering her face with her hands. The silence was broken when Theresa was the first one to jump up and wrap her arms around Mayee to comfort her.

Patricia and Monica looked on in admiration as Theresa kept saying to Mayee,

"Shhhh, it's okay. You didn't do anything wrong girl. You didn't do anything wrong."

Patricia felt that there was definitely more to what was being said. Than just a quick fuck or a simple one night affair. Patricia's eyes began to water as she got up from the couch pointing at Mayee and Theresa saying,

"I wanna know what the fuck is going on? And I want to know now!"

Monica repeating the statement saying

"Yeah, we wanna know right now, Mayee!"

Theresa was facing Mayee with her back to Patricia and Monica. She signaled Mayee with her eyes to keep quiet and not let them know that Nathan was abusing her.

Mayee blinked her teary eyes and removed Theresa's hands from her face gritted her teeth and said,

"No! That's enough. That's it. I can't take anymore of this shit!"

"Who's shit?" Patricia asked.

"Nathan's shit?" Monica stated as she continued. "And if he cheated on you, then why should you feel guilty for cheating on his ass?" Asked Monica rolling her eyes.

"He's not cheating on her, as far as we know Monica." Theresa said looking down at the floor.

"If that's not it, then what's the problem?" Patricia asked in a sarcastic tone.

"He beats me,"

She said with her voice cracking.Patricia and Monica faces froze as if time had suddenly stood still. It even seemed like for a second or two, that the fish in Mayee's aquarium had stopped swimming in their graceful circular motion. It was so quiet you could hear everyone's heart beating. Patricia turned to Theresa,

"Did you know about this?"

Theresa looked at Mayee and placed her pinky finger in her mouth biting the tips of paint on her nail with one eyebrow raised up.

"It's okay, Theresa," Mayee said.

"You fucking Bitch! How could you keep some shit like that from me? Of all people!" Patricia shouted at Theresa.

"Wait a minute, Pat," Mayee said.

"No Fuck that!" Patricia shouted and turned to Monica to start on her.

"And how the fuck can you sit there and not say anything, Monica?"

"Wait the fuck up Hoe. Don't even bring that shit over here, Pat."

Theresa looked at Mayee and said,

"See why I told you to keep that shit quiet."

Mayee screamed at the top of her lungs, "Stop!"

Patricia and Monica shut up and folded their arms facing away from each other. Mayee got up from her seat and walked over to Patricia and Monica then grabbed both of their faces squeezing their cheeks softly and told them to stop it in a girly tone with a smile on her face.

"Come on! We've been girls since our first piece of dick. I need y'all to help me now. I need all of you. I thought Nathan was just going through a phase because the pressure of being a lawyer was a serious task. I told Theresa because if I had told all three of you I was afraid you all would have over done it like you are doing now. But it's started getting worse."

"How many times?" Patricia asked.

"First he hit me once or twice in the first two years. But the last year, since we got engaged, he's been hitting me for every little fucking thing. He hits me if I answer him in a loud tone. He hits me if I don't answer fast enough. He fucking hits me if I'm on my Goddamn period. Just a month ago, that mother fucker hit me just to wake me up. What scares me and keeps me from pressing charges is that he has everybody in his pocket. The police won't go near him because he's won more lawsuits against the NYPD than Johnny Cochran. He's even been threatening to ruin my credit if I try to leave him. You've seen him on TV. He knows everybody!"

Monica reached for her purse to get her cell phone out.

"Well he don't know my cousin Milo from Story Ave."

"You talking about that fine ass cousin Geoff?" Patricia asked smiling.

"Yeah that's my heart. He's straight up street. I know he's done two state bids out there bussing his gun off. But he don't play that hitting women shit."

"No Monica! I heard your aunt say he's doing real good now. Isn't he writing books or something like that?" Patricia asked.

"Yeah, Monica, leave that man alone. We can figure this out." Theresa said.

The four of them were just sitting around for a few minutes when they were startled by the doorbell. Mayee jumped up and started to fix herself up quickly.

"Oh shit!"

"Oh shit what?" Theresa asked.

"Who's that? Nathan?" Monica asked Mayee silently.

"Hell no! That's Kevin!"

"Kevin?" Patricia asked.

"Yes!"

They all scurried around bumping into each other trying to fix the place up in seconds.

"Why didn't you tell us that brother was coming?" Patricia asked.

"What the hell is wrong with you Mayee?" Theresa asked.

"That's what's up!" said Monica laughing.

"Chill out and don't get crazy!" Mayee said pointing at them all.

She walked to the door checking her face and hair. She pushed her tits up and opened the door.

CHAPTER VI

"FACE OFF"

A MAN IS NOT DEFINED BY HIS ACTIONS, BUT BY HIS CHARACTER. AND HIS CHARACTER IS NOT DEFINED BY HIS VALUES BUT BY HIS MORALS. AND HIS MORALS ARE NOT DEFINED BY HIS FAILURES BUT BY HIS VICTORIES. AND HIS VICTORIES ONLY DEFINE SUCCESS!

Milo's Quote

The Cabbie pulled up in front of Mayee's house after he had driven around the same block five times. I knew that he was trying to get more money out of me even after I had agreed to give his grimy ass an extra $20 for his time. If there is one thing that pisses me off the most, it's when a mother fucker tries to play mind games. That's when you find out who the fuck Kevin really is. I didn't start out driving a Cadillac Escalade, so what made him think that I didn't know the price from Manhattan to Queens was $35 plus the toll. If he had gotten me there faster I was going to bless him with a fifty plus the regular fare.

So I opened the car door, walked to the driver's window, leaned in and said to him, "Now what if I walk the fuck off because you tried some slick bullshit?"

"I don't know what is it you say, I'ze a take you to dis address,"

The cabbie answered with an African accent.

I told him that he was a funny ass dude as I pulled a whole stack of $100 bills out of my pocket. I peeled one off the top and threw it on his lap. I shook my head and started to walk up Mayee's walkway. Before I pressed the doorbell, I took a minute to see how big her house was. I thought to myself, "Damn", it's time to step my game up. Her house was beautiful. The landscape was amazing. I didn't even notice the big ass weeping willow tree with one of those homemade swings with the 2 x 4 and thick ropes hanging from a branch. Her door must have been at least 10 feet tall and 5 feet wide.

After I had done the Harlem shake, because I knew Mayee had her own money, or came from a family with money, I finally pressed the bell.

Mayee fumbled with the lock and opened the door. There she was, in the flesh, standing there staring at me with her pretty squinted eyes. She was wearing a tank top with her sorority symbol on the front. It was a gym sports bra that women work out in. She had on a pair of black sweat spandex shorts on. It didn't do much to hide the shape of where a woman's private part or gap might be. The shorts hugged tightly, and outlined everything. Her hair was in a high ponytail giving the effect of a horse's tail. Once again all I could say was,

"Damn"! You are so fine."

"Oh Kevin, please come on in."

She pulled my arm sleeve, dragged me in and, to my surprise, there were three other woman that looked just ass fine as she did. Being the outspoken person I've always been, I couldn't help but say,

"What in the fisheezee! I swear there's got to be some secluded island out there that breeds nothing but fine sistah's like y'all."

"Kevin please don't start them up, because you will have to keep that up the whole stay here." Mayee said taking my coat and hat.

"Hi, I'm Patricia, that's Monica and Theresa. Now, what was you saying about how fine we are?"

Everybody started to giggle. And insisted that I get comfortable and to make myself feel at home. I sat down on Mayee's love seat checking out the pictures in her wall unit. That's where I saw Mayee in a photo with a woman. I knew it was her mother. She was pure Japanese. it threw me for a moment. I noticed that most of the furniture and picture frames were oriental and appeared to be crafted in Japan.

Mayee asked me what I wanted to drink. Liquor or soda? I told her soda. Because it was too late to start drinking. I was under the impression that her mother might be in the house as well. Monica came out of the kitchen and handed me my drink. She sat down beside me, but not too close. I could tell that these were mature woman. Not the ghetto stereotypes at all. Patricia, who was sitting on the long couch across from us with her legs up, reached for an Essence Magazine from under the living room table. She opened the pages. I thought she was reading them, until I noticed that she was staring with her eyes fixed on my face. I smiled and took a sip from my glass, but cut my eyes towards the kitchen waiting for Mayee to rescue me from the uncomfortable feeling. Monica started small conversation with me. Nothing real specific, just idle chat. We talked for about 10 minutes.

When we had stopped for a second, Patricia cut in quickly,

"So Kevin do you have a small or big family? Sisters? Brothers?"

"I have a younger sister. How about you Patricia?" I shot back because of the way she had asked.

"Yes I have two sisters at home. But I consider Mayee my blood. We've known each other forever. I hope you don't think I'm coming at you sideways? It's just that--."

"Yeah I know. You wanna know what type of man I am. I'm sure out of concern for Mayee," I said politely.

Mayee and Theresa came out of the kitchen with a bowl of Buffalo Wings and French Fries. Monica got up so Mayee could take her place beside me. Mayee stated how hungry she was and started to chow down on the wings first. I crossed my legs and placed Mayee's back against my chest. She took a wing and placed it at my lips, and asked do I want a bite. I shook my head no and smiled. I couldn't take it anymore. The silence. The eyes. The whole shit made me feel like I was under a fucking microscope. I'm far from stupid, and I damn sure ain't your simple ass brother who don't know the difference from being accepted or rejected. I asked Mayee if she could please show me to the bathroom. She wiped her hands with her napkin, grabbed my hand, and told them she'll be back.

As we exited the living room heading towards the staircase, I heard Patricia clearly say,

"We'll be right here, just shout if you need us, okay?"

"I said I'll be back Patricia!" Mayee paused and rolled her eyes.

I was under the impression she had told them about that morning, and what had happened between us. I asked myself, "Did she say that I had gotten rough with her? Did she tell them I had done some kind of harm to her? And if so, why would she invite me over?"

We reached the top of the stairs, made a left and passed three bedrooms until we came to the bathroom door. The door was already open. She turned on the light and walked me over to the sink.

She grabbed the back of my head and stuck her soft tongue down my throat. She pulled on my zipper and stuck her hand down my pants and massaged my dick.

"I've been going crazy thinking about you Kevin. Mmmm, touch me Kevin. Oh, please touch me."

"Wait a minute Mayee." I whispered. She was definitely turning me on.

"No baby. I want you to take me now baby." Mayee had that sad puppy dog face on.

"Mayee. Please I have to ask you something right now!"

She placed her head in the center of my chest. Then she placed both hands in my back pockets and asked me what was wrong.

"I don't know what the hell is going on. But I know there's something you should be telling me. I can feel it in the air. And I'm very concerned about you Mayee." I said with a serious face.

She took both hands out of my pockets and sat on the toilet seat.

"If you're talking about that morning, you're right. I do have a lot of explaining to do. I owe you that Kevin."

Before she started to tell me the reason for her emotional outburst, the doorbell rang unexpectedly. Mayee's eyes almost popped right out of their sockets. I gave her a look that warned her I was beginning to feel uneasy. She got up from the toilet seat in somewhat of a slow motion manner placing one hand over her heart. She put the other hand up facing me as she signaled me to stay right there. She walked out of the bathroom. The doorbell rang again and again. I knew it was on and popping. I still had my 9 mm gun stuffed in the arch of my back under my shirt. I was surprised that she hadn't felt it there at all. Then I heard it all begin from the moment she opened the door.

I recognized Patricia's voice from the sound.

"Nah nigga, don't be coming all up in here like you the fucking man up in this bitch! We know about your sorry woman beating ass!"

I could hear Theresa's voice, because she had a raspy type scratching sound whenever spoke.

"Nathan, I don't think you should be here. Me and you have been through this before and you know I'm not afraid of you at all. First it was just me, but now there are four of us and I don't think you can handle all of us at once!"

I had no idea what he looked like, his size, his weight. All I could hear was his voice and from what I heard him say, I knew the shit was about to hit the fan.

"Listen, you bitches need to mind your business and let me handle mine. I'm fucking Mayee. I'm not fucking any one of you. What happens between me and my fiancé is our business. Besides, if she leaves me, not only will I crush her, but I'll crush you too. And all of your families as well. Men run shit in this world. And if we didn't let you bitches climb the ladder, where would y'all be?"

I heard Monica's response to his crazy ass statement,

"Oh hell fucking no! You gotta go! You get the fuck out Nathan! Get the fuck out NOW!"

As I waited agitated and restless in that bathroom, I kept thinking that I should make my presence known to this punk ass dude right now no matter what Mayee wanted. I tried to keep my composure for just a little while longer. I'm not sure what was happening downstairs but it sounded like Monica tried to push him out the door. I could hear the scuffling of shoes on the floor. Then I heard a loud thud. Like when someone falls off of a bed and hits the floor real hard. Mayee screamed.

"No! Please Stop! These are my friends Nathan! Leave them alone!"

That was it. This mother fucker was acting crazy. I needed to get this shit over with. I checked my gun, threw some cold water on my face, looked in the mirror and said to myself, "Yeah, this nigga got to go!" I opened the door and headed in the direction of all the commotion. I had to end this shit right now.

While they were arguing and shoving each other around, in silence I walked down the stairs with my gun behind my back. When I reached the bottom of the stairs, I could see Theresa and Patricia with their fists balled up ready to get it on with Nathan. Mayee was squatting and hugging Monica on the floor next to the wall unit. Everyone turned their heads in my direction: Mayee, Monica, Patricia, Theresa, and this dude named Nathan.

Patricia shouted out while pointing her fingers at Nathan, "Yeah nigga, now what!"

Nathan pointed his finger at me while looking at Mayee and smiling.

"Who the fuck is this wannabe fake ass thug-looking mother fucker?"

I couldn't believe my eyes. Nathan was 6' 2" tall, skinny as hell, wearing a blazer some jeans and some nice fucking shoes. We all know how that story goes. It's always the no heart, no street knowledge, quiet ass brothers that have all the money but no real balls. The only way they can really get a nut off is, by finding some woman they can try to dominate because they got tons of baggage from getting their asses handed to them on a regular during their childhood years. But I was as cool as a fan.

"Who the fuck is he Mayee?"

"Why don't you ask me? I'm standing right here," I said smoothly.

"Okay, then who the fuck are you?"

"I'm the one who's going to free your mind."

I love The Matrix movies. So much sometimes without skipping a beat its dialogue that just pops out of my mouth.

"Free my mind?" Nathan asked puzzled.

Everyone was staring at me as though I was fucking crazy. But I never took my eyes off of Nathan. I don't even think I blinked since I found myself standing on that spot.

"Sounds to me like you've lost your mind Homie."

Nathan began to take a step in my direction. But before he could get closer, I pulled the gun from behind my back and raised it up and pointed it directly in the center of his forehead. Nathan froze immediately without the slightest hesitation. If you have never had the experience of a gun being pointed directly at you, when it happens, believe me it will make you stop all the grinning and laughing and bullshit.

"Wait a minute, Kevin."

Mayee said sounding frightened.

"Yeah, wait a minute. K...K...Kevin." Nathan stuttered.

"No! We don't have a minute Mayee. How many minutes do you need? How many minutes does it take him to finish beating you? How many minutes does it take for the pain and the swelling to go away? Besides my love, I only need one second."

I pulled the hammer back on the gun and I still didn't blink. Nathan swallowed spit and began to back away real slowly.

"You know if you shoot me Kevin I have witnesses."

"Really?" I said with a halfhearted smile.

"Let's see what we have here Mr. Big Time Lawyer. First, you force your way into your fiancée's house. Secondly, not to mention abusing Mayee. You attacked her friend physically. Threw her to the ground and in your jealous rage you come up the stairs to attack me because you thought she was cheating on you. Not to mention the large amount of drugs in your car that the cops will find while you are in the ER getting the bullets pulled out of your ass."

"I don't deal drugs!"

Nathan said looking puzzled again.

"You're not liked by the NYPD very much Mr. Nathan, Nathan Livingston, if I'm correct? I know all about you. If you ask me, your commercials fucking suck! You sorry ass piece of shit. Half the Crime Lords that pay you only use your ass to stay out of jail. But what you don't know is half these niggas work for my peoples. And those people owe me a lot of favors. So, this is how this is going to play out. Mayee's going to ask you to leave so we can get our fuck on. Mayee ask him to leave please?"

Mayee looked at me blinking really fast. Patricia's mouth was wide open and she was standing real still while Monica and Theresa had their hands over their mouths. Nathan stared at Mayee with a look of disbelief waiting for her response.

"Nathan, please get out of my house! Please just leave and take your ring with you. I'm not marrying you ever!"

Mayee took the ring off of her finger and threw it at him. Nathan picked up the ring looked at me and walked to the door, opened it, then left Mayee's house. I closed the hammer on the gun, put it back in my pants and walked to the couch and sat down. I crossed my legs in a real cool way.

"Now where were we, ladies?"

Monica hopped up off the floor and started to jump up and down in one spot. "Oh shit! Oh shit! Oh shit! Kevin's a "G", Kevin's a G-G-G-G-G Unit!"

"You go Mayee with your platinum pussy!" Patricia said grabbing her own tits.

"I can't believe that just happened?" Theresa said sitting back down on the couch.

Mayee folded her arms and started to cry. I gave her a huge hug and told her I was sorry to bring that kind of drama in her house. She said it wasn't that. It was that she knew that this situation wasn't over, and that Nathan wasn't going to let things go down that easily. He would somehow find a way to get revenge on her. She was worried about what I would do next. I told her that I go with situations day-by-day. Then Theresa told the girls to get their things because we needed to have some time alone. The girls got their things together walked over to me and all three of them gave me a big group hug. I was shocked to even still be in Mayee's house after all that had gone down. They said their goodbye's while me and Mayee cuddled on the couch and watched them leave.

"Why did you do that, Kevin?"

"I don't know Mayee. But I do know all that shit made my dick hard." I said smiling.

Mayee laughed and we went up to her room.

CHAPTER VII

"IT'S A SMALL WORLD"

"Livingston & Teller. The lawyers you can trust. Do you have trouble getting the money you deserve? Well, Livingston & Teller are the lawyers you should call. Livingston & Teller have been fighting for the people for 10 years. And we've gotten their cases settled: for the people! for the money! and for you! Call (212) 555-6767. Livingston & Teller are waiting."

Nathan Livingston and his partner Brandon Teller clapped their hands after watching their new commercial presentation on a large movie screen positioned in their conference room on the forty-fifth floor of their law firm located on Water Street. Nathan has been working for Brandon and his father, Sheldon Teller, for fifteen years. Sheldon

Teller had made him partner 10 years ago before he passed away from lung cancer.

Nathan had been born within a privileged lifestyle. His family was very wealthy and made their money during the early '50s. Nathan's great-grandfather had been one of the first African-Americans to become a judge. Nathan's great-great-grandparent's ancestry crossed genes with Booker T. Washington in the late 19th Century when Booker T. Washington had founded the Tuskegee Institute in eastern Alabama. This bloodline helped to lay the foundation under which Nathan's family positioned itself: with a focus always on the vigilant pursuit of education and skill aptitude. To a large extent, something which Booker T. Washington believed black people should be provided with. With all the education and wealth that Nathan had been provided with, he had allowed modern times to transform him into an individual with an uncontrollable, duality lifestyle.

"I hope you liked the presentation," a blonde-haired heavyset woman said sitting across the large oakwood table that sat fifteen people. There were only five of them watching the presentation, however.

"I would like to thank you and the advertising agents who worked so hard at putting that sorry ass commercial together ladies and gentlemen."

The blonde-haired lady smiled and said, "Thank you for your time." Being the only woman in the room, she knew that Nathan had been cracking on her weight. Three of the agents grabbed their briefcases and CD's and left the conference room.

"Nathan, what has gotten into you?" Brandon asked.

"What? Come on, Brandon?"

"Nathan!" Brandon shouted as he slammed his hand down on the table.

"Damn Brandon, okay. I'll call them back and say I'm sorry. Would that make you feel better about spending a million dollars to have our commercial shown during the Super Bowl? That commercial was shit!"

"Okay Nathan, you got a point there. But did you see the size on that girl? I'll bet she made a ton of money doing Burger King commercials, get it?"

Nathan and Brandon burst out laughing for a few seconds until the conference room door opened. Sharon, the secretary walked over to Nathan and handed him a folder. She was wearing a red two-piece Gucci blazer and matching skirt with Gucci flats on her feet. Sharon was a petite and very sexy young black woman with shoulder length hair dyed burgundy. Nathan and Brandon had their hands up to their faces while sitting back in their two leather chairs.

"What's this Sharon?" said Nathan, who sized her up while taking the folder from her.

"This is one of the cases that Ms. Dawson asked me to show you." She said, while smiling at him.

""Oh shit! I completely forgot about Ms. Dawson. Tell her I'll be right there in a minute and please tell Gene Dawson that she's my sweetheart and I'm sorry, okay?"

"Yes, Mr. Livingston, I'll tell her immediately,"

"You know Gene Dawson has been here just as long as I have, Brandon?"

"So what are you saying, Nathan? I think it's about that time to add a new partner. What do you think?"

"Gene's been working here way before she became a lawyer. It was my father who helped pay for some of her education when I was just learning about the business. She used to wipe my running nose when I was a little boy playing in this same conference room almost 30 years ago."

Brandon had a big smile on his face while he was reminiscing about his father. Ms. Dawson had played a part in his upbringing even though he was white and she was black. Brandon's mother was a money-hungry greedy ass bitch, period!

"Yes, I agree Nathan. It's time to let Gene get her share." said Brandon.

"Alright then, let's not tell her until we set up the party plan." Nathan answered.

Gene Dawson was sitting at her desk at the corner office that had a huge window view facing lower Manhattan's harbor. Her desk was all glass with a solid oak base. On her desk, with her little decorative doo-dads, was an expensive laptop. She liked to collect items from various vacations that she had taken. Trips to the Bahamas, Jamaica, and European locales. In addition to a few one-of-a-kind fertility statues from Africa. Her prized possession was a couple of pictures of herself, Kevin, and her daughter Keisha enjoying a few family outings. Although she only talked to Sharon about her personal life, she was most proud of her son. Kevin Dawson.

While Gene gazed at her pictures, Sharon walked into her office causing a distraction which snapped her out of her momentary reverie.

"What's up, Girl?" Gene asked Sharon.

"What's wrong, Sharon?" she asked again.

"Nothing" Sharon answered looking away.

"Now Sharon you need to stop that. If anybody knows your ass, it's me."

"I hate the way Nathan looks at me. He gives me the fucking creeps!"

"Now we both know he thinks he's so goddamn fine girl. Please don't even get bent out of shape over his bullshit."

"I know Gene. So what's up with Kevin? I'm not asking because he took me out a couple of times and never tried to get any. I just sincerely miss him." said Sharon smiling playfully.

"Right, right Sharon. Uh huh. I know, sincerely miss him."

"I do!"

"I told you Kevin won't get serious with my secretaries. He thinks that would be disrespectful."

"Well, can you tell him I'm having a party next weekend and not to bring that horny-ass Kurt with him?"

"Okay, I'll do that for you Sharon."

"Anyway, Nathan said he'll be with you in a few minutes and you're still his sweetheart, some shit like that."

"Thanks sweetie."

Sharon left Gene's office so she could continue with her morning runs. A few minutes later Nathan walked into Gene's office holding a rose behind his back.

He walked towards her quoting P. Diddy's catchy phrase, "I thought I told ya that we won't stop! I thought I told ya that we won't stop!" Nathan danced all the way to Gene's desk. He sat down at the corner of the desk and placed the rose on her laptop. "I'm sorry sweetness. I've been going through some personal problems with my fiancé and I forgot all about the Morgan case. Do you forgive me?"

"Come on, Nathan, I bet that shit works on her." Gene answered.

"Nah, not Mayee. I have to give her special attention."

"What did you say her name was?"

"Mayee Kitomaki. Why?"

Gene uncrossed her legs under her desk hitting the edge of the table leg. "No! I-I just heard that-that...umm, last name before?"

Gene tried to get a better grasp on her words as she realized that her son Kevin was talking about her boss. The man she had worked for was the abusive scum that had made Mayee's life a living hell.

"You know that woman who's always on the news? The Japanese chick who works for the UN Sunzu Kitomaki? Well, anyway, that's her daughter."

"Oh, that's right." Gene answered pretending she was surprised.

Nathan got up from the desk with his back facing Gene walked towards the huge glass windows looking out on to Manhattan. Gene took a quick look at her pictures hoping that Nathan wouldn't turn around and notice them.

"I have a surprise for you Gene." Nathan said while staring out the window.

"What's that?"

Gene began to open her desk drawer real slowly trying not to make a sound. She grabbed the pictures of Kevin and placed them in her drawer. She wasn't about to take a chance not knowing if Nathan and Kevin had crossed paths. Just as she closed the drawer Nathan turned around and reached for her hand.

"Come here Gene."

"What is it K...I mean Nathan?"

Nathan paused for a second and looked at Gene with a serious look. For a moment, she had the impression that she had just blown her cover. Nathan peered at Gene then asked her, "Where do you come off thinking you could hide anything from me?"

"What are you talking about, Nathan?"

"Do you think you could ever get over on me Gene?"

Gene stood totally still and swallowed.

"Do you think you could hide from me the fact that you have wanted to become partner for all these years?"

"What?" Gene said surprised.

"That's right, partner. But don't tell Brandon I told you. Come and give me a hug sweetness."

"P-P-Partner?" Gene's eyes started to water. All the hard work over the years had finally paid off. Gene was about to be given the position that would open many doors for her and bring her closer to her goals. Gene forced herself to give Nathan a hug. She wondered how she could be in a difficult position like this at the same she was experiencing the moment she had been waiting for in her professional career. Gene gave Nathan a brief hug, backed away, and shook his hand.

"Remember Sis, don't tell Brandon I told you."

"I won't, Nathan, thank you again."

Nathan calling her "Sis" made Gene's skin crawl even more. She sat down and stared at her cell phone. It was time for lunch with Kevin.

Chapter VIII

"Decisions Decisions"

The time on the clock was 2:30 p.m. at the police station on 151st between Broadway and Amsterdam Avenue. Kurt was pulled over for suspicion of trafficking narcotics. He was sitting on a hard wooden bench waiting to be booked and finger printed. He was kept separated from the other perps because he was known for his powerful of influence over the local small time dealers. Influence enough to make them take responsibility for his crimes. Most of them worked for him anyway and knew that they could get paid a lot more for doing a small bid of time for Kurt. It had once been said that he had paid a younger brother $175,000 to do 1½-3 year bid. That's $10,000 a month. Shit, you do the math.

Kurt sat there as calm as ever looking like he was waiting to be interviewed by Ebony Magazine. He even had the nerve to ask a female officer who was working behind her desk if she was getting enough dick at home and if she ever needed to get away for a weekend he would be happy to give her both. Some dick and a vacation. The sister gave Kurt the middle finger and continued to type away while Kurt smiled and said that he had meant no offense. He was just keeping it real.

Actually, Kurt was arrested at 8:00 a.m. that morning. The practice was that the arresting undercover officers would have someone like Kurt sit for many hours trying to break their resistance hoping that they would start to give up information in exchange for a release. Kurt was no amateur at playing the game. So instead of his resistance being broken, he continued to give the police a run for their money. Besides, there had been no drugs found in his possession. He knew something was going on. But he couldn't put his finger on what it might be.

Undercover Police Officer Juan Sanchez took the handcuffs off and walked Kurt to his desk to begin processing.

"So, Officer Sanchez, how much do you make a year again... $35,000? $45,000? Why do you do it?"

"Because at my age, I don't get as much pussy as you do nowadays." Sanchez answered as he began to write Kurt's name on the case file.

"Come on Sanchez, the last time I saw you and your wife we happened to be eating at the same restaurant on City Island. And she was fine as hell. No disrespect."

"None taken Kurt. That was two years ago. She's gotten so fat now I have to roll her in flour to find the wet spot."

"That's some cold shit Sanchez. I'm gonna take you to the Bahamas and get you some ass. So you can chill out for a while." Kurt leaned back and crossed his legs to get comfortable.

"Kurt, your money is so dirty. Ask me how dirty your money is?"

"How dirty is my money Sanchez?"

"Your money is so dirty that the last time we counted it, we thought that Benjamin Franklin was Don King."

"Oh shit!" Kurt burst out laughing holding his stomach and slapping his hand on his knee.

"Oh my God! That was crazy funny. Now tell me why the fuck are we sitting here telling each other jokes?"

"Well Kurt, somebody's rolled over on you and has implicated you. We don't have evidence for drugs or trafficking, but from the confession we've received we can hold you for conspiracy and you will go through the system."

Kurt smiled at Sanchez and took a piece of gum out of his pocket and began to chew smacking it real loud. "That's it? That's all you have is someone's sorry ass confession? Well then I would like to call my lawyers. And Mr. Sanchez, my lawyers are so good you'll be working in Alaska by tomorrow morning. So dress warm my man." Kurt said.

- oOo -

Gene was still sitting at her desk waiting for Kevin to call her for lunch. Her clock flashed 2:45 p.m. She was still in shock since Nathan had left her office after giving her the news about becoming a partner in the firm. She had reached for her cell phone to call Kevin when Nathan came back inside.

"Grab your things, Gene. I need you to take a ride uptown with me. I just got a call from one of my private clients. He's being held for conspiracy and I know they don't have enough proof to put him through the system."

"I'm waiting for a very important phone call. Can you get someone else?"

"No Gene! I need you to get used to going out in the field where the juice is. That's grounds for a civil law suit. Now come on. I have a limo waiting downstairs."

"Don't be talking to me like that Nathan! I'm not one of your hoochie mamas boy."

"Okay Gene, I'm sorry. Please can you go with me then? Because you're going to be partner and I want to give this one to you."

"In that case, let's go kick some ass."

The limo pulled up in front of the police station where Gene and Nathan stepped out with their expensive clothes and briefcases to match. Nathan opened the door for Gene to walk through as they both walked to the front desk. Gene asked to speak to the Captain immediately and demanded to see her client. Captain Stanley came from a room behind the desk while eating a doughnut.

"You can't be serious?" Captain Stanley said, when he saw Nathan's face.

Nathan handed Gene the folder out of his briefcase while smiling at Captain Stanley.

"Mr. Livingston is not your problem Captain Stanley. I am, if you don't release my client in less than five minutes."

"And you are?" Captain Stanley asked.

"Gene Dawson of Livingston, Teller and Dawson."

"Well, Ms. Dawson. I understand who you are now, but it doesn't work that fast. First, you have to let me know who your client is?" Captain Stanley said sarcastically.

Gene opened the folder trying not to look unprofessional because she hadn't been briefed on the way to the station. She read the name so fast that she didn't realize at first who it was.

"Kurt Smith and I hope he's in one piece Captain Stanley."

"Oh, Kurt Smith, it figures. I'll go in the back and set up a room for you to speak to Mr. Smith. Excuse me, Ms. Dawson, but please once again, you are going to follow the correct procedures."

Nathan's cell phone rang allowing Gene time to do a quick scan of Kurt's file. Gene walked over to the soda machine that was in the far corner near the restroom and a dirty water fountain. Gene was thinking. "what harm could it do if Nathan found out that Kurt and Kevin were best friends." Gene snapped out of that thought, grabbed her blazer, brushed it off and began to straighten up while thinking to herself, "I'm a grown ass woman. I'm here to do my job. Whatever is going on between them is a man thing."

"Ms. Dawson, Mr. Smith is in Room 3 down the hall on your left." One of the police officers screamed out.

Nathan ended his phone call when he heard the officer shout. He walked up to Gene and commented. "Let's go see our client." They both entered Room 3 where Kurt was sitting at a table drinking some hot tea and smoking a cigarette.

"Hey, Momma Gene what the fuck...I mean what are you doing here?" Kurt jumped up quickly pulling a seat out for her.

Nathan's face fell flat. All expression gone as he stared at Gene as she took a seat by Kurt.

"Yo Nathan you can sit your own ass down. Excuse me Momma Gene. But what the fuck took you so long?"

"Kurt Smith show some respect to my co-worker Mr. Livingston and stop cussin' so much."

"You work for Mr. Livingston? I thought you were here for support Momma Gene."

"I am Kurt. Now that I know it's you I'm representing. But you have to keep it professional and businesslike so please call me Ms. Dawson."

Nathan unbuttoned his blazer, crossed his legs and folded his hands and placed them over his knee. Nathan then asked, "May I ask where you two know each other from?"

Kurt looked at Gene from the corner of his eye and could see her put the folder down on the table with a "thud," just enough for Kurt to know that it was the family signal for shut your mouth. Don't tell Nathan too much.

"Ms. Dawson helped one of my female cousins get out of a court settlement and she's been a family friend ever since. But like she said, let's keep it professional okay?"

"Well then, shall we?" Nathan asked and continued to let Gene question him about the reasons they had arrested him.

They sat for about an hour before it was concluded that the police did in fact have a case, but a small one that could be settled in court if Kurt was represented correctly. If not, he was sure to spend some time in prison. Gene had posted bail for $10,000 and Kurt was released into their custody with an appearance scheduled in Manhattan Supreme Court in two months.

Walking out of the police station Kurt's Lexus was parked in the police station's lot and the limo was on its way.

"So Momma, I mean Ms. Dawson, I'll call you later and tell Kevin to give me a call. I was on my way to see him about some shit he got into over this chick last night. He left a long message on my cell. But those officers killed my day."

Kurt gave Gene a hug while Nathan pretended not to hear their private goodbye conversation. Nathan turned his head away and gritted his teeth while Gene's head was over Kurt's shoulder. She did the same. Kurt had no idea of what he had just done, or the damage that could follow.

"Yo Nathan I'll call too." Kurt said with his lips turned up being disrespectful.

"Hey Kurt, let me walk you to your car. I have some other business to discuss."

"Yeah whatever." Kurt answered.

"Umm Gene, I'll be right back."

Gene nodded okay, crossed her arms and looked down the street to see if the limo was coming. Nathan and Kurt walked to his car. Kurt unlocked the door then got in and Nathan sat in the passenger's seat slamming the door real hard.

"Yo what the fuck is wrong with you nigga? Are you on some shit slamming my door like that?"

Nathan was surely crazy for pulling a stunt like that normally. But being that the ball was now in his court, he knew he could find out about Kevin through Kurt.

"No, you listen to me now, punk! I'm that mother fucker your boy Kevin has a beef with. I knew this shit would soon work its way to me. And if you want me to keep your ass out of prison you'll do what I say and how I say. And I'll tell you how I'm going to stop that 5-10 sentence from being handed down for conspiracy." Kurt could see the fear in Nathan's eyes and his right hand was trembling as he tried to be all tough.

"What the...? Oh, I get it now. Kevin's got his dick down your girl's throat and you're taken that shit all personal." Kurt said with a big grin.

"Yeah, real personal. Now here's what I want you to do."

"First of all, you bitch ass hatin' mother fucker. Kevin's been my boy for 33 years and you think I'll turn on him because my lawyer threatens to let me go to jail?"

"Oh you'll go alright Kurt. Now like I was saying..." Nathan proceeded to tell Kurt what he wanted. Meanwhile, Gene was getting a little worried about what was taking so long. As she started to get out of the limo Nathan approached the car door.

"This has been an interesting day. We can go now," said Nathan with a disturbing smile while getting into the limo.

Gene put a false smile on her face and the limo driver pulled off.

CHAPTER IX

"MUST CONQUER YOUR FEARS"

FACT: In America, a woman is physically abused every 12-15 seconds by either her husband or boyfriend.

A month has passed since Mayee told Nathan the relationship was over. During that time, Nathan continued leaving messages trying to convince her to come over and try to work things out between them. She never returned any of his calls. She tried her hardest to stay away from Nathan until her mother Sunzu questioned her during dinner that night.

"Mayee?"

"Yes mother?"

"I was thinking about your strange behavior lately and why are you not wearing your family's jade bracelet?"

"Come on Mom. I've always been strange to you. That's because we live in different times now and you are so old fashioned."

"I'm not totally old fashioned. I like that rapper Jay-C...Jay-K...oh, I know Jay-Z!"

They both laughed and continued to eat. After they were finished, they sat down by the fireplace. Sunzu started to brush her hair like she used to do when she was a little girl.

"I know you're in a bad space. Do you want to talk about it?"

"Ma, I can't believe how stupid I was to stay with Nathan after he had treated me like I was a piece of shit."

"Well we all have our demons to face sooner or later. I just hope you didn't leave the family heirloom over at Nathan's house."

Sunzu was still brushing her hair when she realized how quiet her daughter had become when she asked her again about the bracelet.

"Mayee? Mayee Kitomaki! Where is that bracelet?" she said anxiously. Sunzu pushed Mayee's head off her lap with sudden force. She then abruptly jumped up and angrily repeated.

"Mayee! I can't believe you could do something so stupid! That bracelet is not only insured, it has been passed down through this family for eight generations. Japan has a spiritual connection to every piece of jewelry, stone, sword and cloth! Do you know what my mother had to go through when she lied to my father about giving it to me? Do you?!!

"Mommy, I'm sorry,"

Her eyes filling up with tears.

"Sorry!! Dammit! Go and get that bracelet! Do you hear me? You go and get that bracelet now!"

"I'm scared! Ok! I'm scared of him!! Mayee screamed out as she slammed her hands on the carpet and began to weep uncontrollably.

"Why are you afraid of Nathan Livingston? What's going on my daughter?" stunned by her daughter's sudden outburst.

"He's a horrible person Mom. He's not what you or the public thinks he is. He beats his women. He has beaten me Mom, several times."

"Oh my God! I had no idea. Why didn't you tell me these things? Oh my God! Have we not been that close in the past five years?"

"Mom, you work at the UN and I didn't want your career jeopardized by your daughter's personal mess. Which would surely bring the press straight to your door."

"You are correct about that. Those press and paparazzi people are crazy. My God, they questioned a mouse one time in the UN because someone had dressed it up in a suit and put it on the stage as a joke." Sunzu said while trying to relieve Mayee's fear.

Mayee got up and hugged her mother as they began to laugh out loud. Sunzu lifted up Mayee's face with both hands and look intently into her eyes.

"Honey, you have to get that bracelet. I'm going with you."

"Mom, I don't want both of us getting beat up."

"You see why I told you Kung Fu is not just an art but a defense against attackers? Shit! I'll kick his ass all up and down. Oh my goodness, did I just curse?"

"Mommy, I know you didn't just say that! Besides it's time to face my fears anyway. I'll go and get the stun gun just in case, for extra protection."

She gave her mother another hug and went upstairs to change her clothes. She put on some sweats, a pair of sneakers, put her hair in a bun, and grabbed the stun gun from her drawer. She was contemplating calling Kevin for some back up. She thought against it. So instead, she just took her cell.

Taking her mother's car keys to the Mercedes Benz, she then made her way to the garage.

While pulling out of the garage, Mayee's hands were trembling. All she could think of was, that Nathan was sure to put his hands on her because of the way he was embarrassed when Kevin pulled a gun on him. On the drive to Nathan's condo in Manhattan, she kept reminding herself to stay focused and not to be weak or scared. She finally arrived in front of Nathan's building, double-parked, and told the doorman José that she was going upstairs to Nathan's penthouse to grab a few things that she had left behind. José walked her to the elevator put the key in the slot and pressed the top floor button.

"José, do you know if Nathan is in today?"

"I'm not sure Ms. Kitomaki. I just got in for the shift change."

"Well anyway, thank you, José."

"You're welcome, Ms. Kitomaki."

She put her hand on the stun gun keeping a tight grip on it as the elevator made its ascent. As the elevator reached its destination and the door opened, she sneaked a quick peek around the corner to see if Nathan was anywhere in sight. So far the place appeared empty. She walked into the living room area and real quietly glanced up at Nathan's bedroom loft. She didn't see Nathan in his room, so she quickly ran up the stairs trying to get to her jewelry box on the dresser near the window. She opened the box hurriedly knocking over a picture of her and Nathan having dinner at one of the firm's parties.

She picked up the picture and began to search the box for her bracelet. She was relieved to see it still there under all of the other pieces of jewelry. Earrings, necklaces, and a few diamonds. Including the diamond ring she had thrown at Nathan. She grabbed the jade bracelet and left all the other items intact. She put the bracelet in her pocket and began to sprint down the stairs. She walked through the living room to the door, when Nathan came from behind her, placing her in a headlock and forcefully shoved her to the floor.

"And where the fuck do you think you're going?"

"Nathan! Just wait a minute!" She cried out as she squirmed backwards toward the couch.

"How many minutes do you need?" Nathan said sarcastically repeating Kevin's words form that night at her house. He was now hovering over Mayee.

"NATHAN!!"

It was too late for her screams to be heard. Nathan wasted no time as he began his attack. He unleashed a rock-solid punch to her face causing the back of her head to slam into the couch. Blood began to gush out of her nose. He punched her a second time with a left hook to the jaw knocking her clear across the room. She was losing consciousness as she struggled to try to pull herself to the door dragging her weak body because her legs felt paralyzed and would not respond.

"Nathan..." she pleaded. Stop! Pleeease stop!!"

Nathan walked over to Mayee's limp body as she slumped facedown on the floor.

"Turn over Bitch!"

Nathan grabbed her by her hair, spun her over on her back, and cruelly placed the heel of his shoe on her mouth and began to taunt her.

"Yeah Bitch. You think you can fucking treat me like shit? Well, taste some real shit! I stepped in some on the way in."

She struggled to shove the heel off her mouth, but could not gather up enough energy. Nathan continued to press his foot in her face. He finally took his foot off and then sat directly on Mayee's stomach while grabbing the back of her head forcing her to look at him face to face.

"Nathan...Nathan...Nathan..." She gasped as she struggled for breath in between her words.

Nathan spit right in her face. Then he mashed her while slamming her head on the hard marble floor.

"Don't start begging now bitch! I'm just getting starting with this shit!"

Nathan got up off her stomach and made his way to the kitchen area. She could hear him rummaging through the silverware drawer. The few minutes she had spent on her back had revived her long enough for her to dig into her pocket for the stun gun. She gritted her teeth with blood in her mouth and began to feel a little strength returning to her battered body.

She whispered to herself, "This mother fucker." Come on mother fucker. That's right, just come on."

She pretended to be weak and helpless on the floor. She knew that Nathan's arrogance had him believing that she would surrender defeat to him like in the past. The same response he was accustomed to when he was abusive.

"Please Nathan. No! Oh God!"

She sobbed and began to act her ass off waiting for the right moment. Nathan always had some stupid dialogue before beating her. And she knew like clockwork he would show his ass. She also knew that whatever move she made now would be a one-and-done proposition for her. Timing was the key.

Nathan returned with a potato peeler in his hand and started.

"You know Mayee, the only reason I chose your ass is because I had never fucked a Japanese bitch before. I was told you bitches were obedient and knew your place in a relationship."

She was holding her stomach while she covered the stun gun with both hands. Nathan stood over her and tossed the potato peeler back and forth hand-to-hand. She looked Nathan in his eyes and smiled. Then she suddenly began to laugh loudly.

"What the fuck are you laughing at bitch?"

The moment Nathan dropped his guard, she lunged at him with the stunner.

"THIS . . . MOTHER FUCKER!" she shouted. In one swift move, before Nathan realized what was happening, Mayee pressed the power button and rammed the stun gun right into his balls.

Bzzzzzz...bzzzzz "Oww...ohh!" bzzzzz...bzzzzz

Nathan dropped to the floor balled up in a fetal position holding his balls. She scrambled up off the floor and with every ounce of her strength, kicked Nathan in the face. Then she stumbled her way to the door. While she tried to run, Nathan somehow grabbed her ankle making her fall forward on her stomach and breasts.

"Oh...shit! Ouch!" (Cough...cough) Nathan still had a hold on her ankle as she struggled to crawl away. She frantically panicked. When she saw the door was only three feet away, she quickly flipped her body over, and while now positioned on her ass, she began wildly kicking her other leg at Nathan's hand to let go.

"Get the fuck off you son of a bitch!" Mayee screamed. She took the stun gun and shocked his hand.

"Awww...You fucking bitch!" Nathan was forced to release his hold on her ankle while he continued to clutch his balls.

She stumbled her way to the end table, then grabbed a lamp and slammed it on Nathan's head. She ran to the door, opened it, and pressed the close door button on the elevator. When she reached into her pocket, she realized the damn bracelet was not there. She put her hand between the doors so it would reopen. She scanned the floor in the living room and spotted it lying beside Nathan's hand as he lay there semiconscious. She ran back into the room so fast that she tripped over her own foot landing right beside Nathan. Then she picked up the bracelet and staggered to the door. Just before she reached the door, bloody and bruised, she turned and looked back at Nathan crumpled on the floor. She thought, "No not yet you son of a bitch." She walked over to him and in that moment as she looked down, she spit on him and kicked him in the head.

"Fuck you, mother fucker!"

Mayee hauled ass back to the elevator. She pressed the "close door button as the elevator descended to the lobby. She was limping a little as she came toward the front desk. Blood was still in her mouth and on her face when she approached José.

José looked at Mayee's face and said to her,

"If you look like that coming down, I can imagine what that fucking asshole looks like upstairs."

She just looked at José with a puzzled look.

"Please girlfriend, you're the only one who finally fought back." José snapped his fingers in a zformation that she interpreted as a signal that he was delighted that she stood up for herself.

"That's right Sister, I didn't see shit. I didn't hear shit. And fuck that piece of shit. O-kayyyyy! Now get going before the lobby gets filled up."

"Thanks José. I won't forget you around the holidays, I promise."

She walked quickly out to her car. She got in and started the engine. She looked out the front window and noticed an orange ticket left between her windshield wipers. She grabbed the ticket and laughed to herself. "Ouch."

She knew she couldn't go back home looking like that so as she pulled off she called Kevin. She was on 85th Street and Kevin was only 10 blocks away.

"Hey Mayee what's up?" Kevin answered because he knew it was her from the caller ID.

"I need to see you now!"

"Damn! I need to see you too baby."

"I just left Nathan's house and he's laying out cold on the floor."

"Oh shit! Did you kill his ass?"

"No Kevin, I just kicked his ass." She said and began to giggle.

"Wait a minute, you kicked his ass? I knew you had that Jackie Chan shit in you. I knew you was fronting."

"For real Kevin, but he got a few shots in. My face is a little bloody and I can't go home yet. My mother will freak out."

"Alright Ms. Jet Li. come on over baby. I'll run you a bubble bath and I'll be waiting for you. Can I ask you a question?"

"Sure Kevin what is it, Boo?"

"Did all that excitement make your pussy wet?"

"Kevin! You are a freak ass nigga. Damn! Of course my pussy is wet for you baby. I'll be right over. Goodbye Kevin."

She hung up the phone with a huge smile on her face. She took the bracelet out of her pocket and placed it where it belonged. Back on her wrist.

FACT: Every year 3 to 4 million women are battered in their own homes. Every year more than 4,000 women are killed by their husbands or lover. (American Psychiatric Association, Psychiatric News, Coalition to Launch Campaign against Domestic Violence, Joan O'Connor, July 3, 1987)

CHAPTER X

"DELIVER THE PACKAGE"

I prepared Mayee's bubble bath as promised. I even went down to the local flower shop and picked up a few dozen roses to spice things up. I plucked two dozen rose petals and placed them on top of the bubbles for her. I made my bed up nice and neat, fluffed some throw pillows, and placed a bowl of scented oils on the end table so that I could give her a rub down. I took off all my clothes, put on my velvet robe and left my doo-rag on because she said it was cute and she loved to see the thug in me sometimes.

I sprayed some Autumn Rain scented potpourri in the air to give it some flavor. Noticing the time, I knew she would arrive in a few minutes. So I grabbed a few CDs out of the rack; some Luther, Genuwine, R Kelly (of course), some Ron Isley, and some Earth Wind & Fire. I'm an Old School boy. I placed them all in the 20 CD holder, closed the door on the system and pressed Track 7 on R Kelly's best hits.

"Seems like you're ready...Baby are you ready...to go all the way?"

I grabbed myself and did a 360° spin and yelled, "That's my shit."

I was surely in the mood for some sex. I find it hard to give women their props, but Mayee had some good ass pussy.

The doorbell rang. She had finally arrived. I pulled myself together and stopped acting like I had never had a piece of ass before. I walked to the door and opened it. She had her hand covering her mouth. I could see the bruises on her left cheek but I tried to remain calm and collected. She walked in.

"Don't even laugh Kevin."

"What makes you think I would laugh?"

"Cause I know I look crazy."

"Boo you just fine, Okay?"

"I wanna kiss you Kevin, but I should go and brush my teeth first. My mouth is yucky."

"Go on in to the bathroom brush your jibs and get in the bath so I can wash your sexy ass."

"Yes my sweet love."

She kissed me anyway. Her lip was bruised a little bit. It was her nose that was red and looked a little bent to the right. I examined her face to see if her nose was broken. But she was fine. Just a bit shaken.

On her way to the bathroom the doorbell rang again. "Who the hell can this be at a time?" I sucked my teeth and told her to continue getting into the bath and I would go and see who it was. I looked through the peephole and saw that it was my sister Kiki standing there in a girly posture. I flung the door open and grabbed her inside real fast.

"What are you doing Kiki?"

"Damn! I came by real quick to give you a shout out Big Brother."

"Kiki, I love you too. But I'm busy."

"Why it smells all good up in here? Oh I guess you're about to get your freak on up in here, huh?"

"That's right Baby Girl. So make it quick."

"Well anyway. April drove me over to say Hi and Mommy said to call her now! She said that your phone is off or something."

"My phone?"

"Well I'm out Bro. And is Kurt here too?"

"Kurt? No why?"

"I could swear I saw his Lexus up the block? But he wasn't in it. Maybe I'm seeing shit. Anyway, I love you and I'll see you later Okay?"

Kiki gave me a kiss and let herself out. I walked over to my phone to check it...no dial tone. I put the phone down and began to check the wall. I thought maybe the plug fell out.

Mayee called for me "Come on baby."

"I'll be right there in a second, Boo!"

I shrugged my shoulders and didn't give the phone another thought.

I entered the bathroom took my bathrobe off and got into the tub with her. Suds were everywhere. She got up and sat down on top of me rodeo style. She put her breasts in my face with suds dripping off her nipples. I began to suck on them softly. She started to moan and rub my face in her breasts. I could feel my dick getting hard from her movements. She grabbed it and slid me inside softly. I could feel the heat inside the walls of her pussy from the water being so hot. I cupped her ass cheeks and bounced her up and down slowly on my dick.

"Stand me up Baby. I want you to take me from behind Kevin."

"No doubt sexy. You know I like to see your ass from the back."

She stood up first grabbing my hand helping me to stand up without slipping in the tub. She put both hands up on the bathroom tile and arched her back spreading both her legs for me to enter. Being that both our bodies were dripping wet, it made my entrance that much easier. I began to pump her from behind watching every facial expression change with every stroke. I began to pump faster and faster. No rough stuff. I just speeded up a bit for her enjoyment.

"Oh my God! Kevin! I'm gonna cum! I'm gonna cum! Keep going, baby!"

Water was splashing everywhere. I could feel myself about to explode in her pussy.

"I'm coming too Baby! Oh yeah! Oh shit! Here I go!"

"Kevin! Oh Kevin!"

We both grabbed each other's hands as we came to a climax. Together we felt each other's creamy release on one another. We breathed heavy at each other for a few minutes. Looking into each other's eyes, we then giggled like two kids scheming to plan something devious. I unplugged the stopper in the tub so that the water level could go down some and we could take a shower and rinse off. After rinsing off, we went into the bedroom to lie down listen to music, and talk about what we expected to happen next. I was always in tune with my senses and suddenly I felt uneasy. My gut started flipping like crazy. The warning signal was off the hook. I turned to Mayee and told her in a whisper to get dressed slowly and quietly.

"What's wrong Kevin?" she whispered.

"Something's not right," I whispered back.

I closed my bedroom door real slow. I began to put on my underwear and jeans quickly. She put her panties and sweats back on as well. The music was still playing in the CD deck covering whatever noise we made hurrying to get dress in the bedroom. Once she and I were fully dressed, I reached under my bed for the secret hidden space where I kept one of my guns but the gun was not there? My other gun was hidden in the living room just in case I couldn't make it to the bedroom.

I was totally compromised. Kurt was the only one who knew my stash spots and I also gave him a copy of my house keys just in case of an emergency. But Kurt wouldn't play like that so I presumed someone must have broken in while I was down at the flower shop and had been waiting for the right time to attack. I checked the phone again and there was still no dial tone.

"Mayee where's your cell phone?" I whispered pushing her to the floor beside the bed.

"I don't know. I think I left it in the glove compartment." She whispered back.

"You've got to be kidding."

"Well, where the hell is your phone?" she whispered a little too loud.

"Shhhh. Never mind smart ass. I'm going to have to go out in the living room, so stay down. I'll be back."

"Kevin! Kevin?" She whispered as I got up to leave the bedroom.

I opened the bedroom door slowly. I leaned against the hallway wall and I could hear movement out in the living room area. I peeked around the corner. (WHAPP!) I was hit right in the face with the back of someone's gun. Before fading into unconsciousness, I saw a man wearing a black knitted face mask. As I fell to the floor I could see two more men dressed all in black also wearing face masks standing behind the man who had hit me.

I woke up about three hours later lying on my couch. I slowly sat up and took a deep breath. I brushed my hand over my forehead to wipe the blood that was there from the impact of the blow. I sat back for a few seconds scanning the room. I could see nothing was missing. I then knew that this had been a professional job. It didn't take long to figure out what they had come for. I knew she was not in the apartment. Nathan had hired someone to kidnap her. But why would they leave me alive? Was the kidnapper just doing his job? I questioned the whole situation for a few minutes as wild thoughts swirled in my head. As I was about to get up, I checked under the couch for my back-up gun. It wasn't in the spot I had placed it in. I glanced to the far corner under the couch and there it was. Lying there as if someone had put it back for me to find. My cell phone was lying beside it.

All of a sudden, the cell phone began to ring. I picked it up and stared at it for a few rings. I flipped it open to answer it.

"Hello."

"Listen to my instructions very very carefully Kevin."

"Yeah, I'm listening."

"This isn't about money. If you want to save Mayee, take public transportation only to the South Street Seaport, Pier 11 and come alone. Be there at 1:00 a.m."

"How much is he paying you... Kurt?"

The voice at the other end went silent for a few seconds. I could hear Mayee's voice in the background begging to be let go.

"It's not about the money Kevin."

"Then what the fuck are you doing man?"

"Nathan has a tight grip on my balls Kevin. If I don't do what he says, he has it set up for me to go to prison for 10-20 years."

"Kurt! Since when do you let some faggot ass bitch nigga get the drop on you?"

"Kevin! I left your ratchet there for a reason. If you could just follow my lead and trust me on this I have a way."

"Fuck you, Kurt! Trust you? Trust you to flip on me after 33 years of jumping in front of bullets. Thirty-three years of my mother taking you in when your crackhead mother tried to sell you for drugs when you was 4 years old? You gave up 33 years of love and support from your boy Kurt!"

"Kevin just hear me out!"

"No Kurt! I'll be there at 1:00 a.m. Just make sure Nathan is there too."

I hung up the phone on Kurt. I couldn't believe my ears. I began to reminisce about the past with Kurt. I broke down and started crying.

After I had sat there for almost an hour crying on and off, I began to see the obvious picture. Nathan was starting to pick at my life from the inside. Kurt would be first. So what else was he up to? I looked at my phone and decided to call Sprint to see what was wrong with my line.

"Hello Sprint? My name is Kevin Dawson and there's something wrong with my line."

"Hold on Mr. Dawson."

"I'm sorry sir your service has been cut off. I'm seeing a $350 bill that hasn't been paid."

"That's impossible ma'am! My bill has been paid up in full every time for the past 10 years. There's got to be a mistake."

"No sir, I'm sure my computer is correct sir."

"No problem miss. Can I just pay it by credit card over the phone?"

"Yes you can Mr. Dawson. How would you like to pay? Discover? Visa?"

"Yes Visa card number 34967221011228."

"Sorry Mr. Dawson, this card number has been reported stolen."

"What? Never mind."

I hung up the phone. I could feel my heart beating wildly through my chest. I then thought to myself, "Oh shit! Kiki . . . Mom."

Grabbing my gun, I looked at the time and saw that I still had time to check on my mother. Kiki had been with her best friend April when she left my apartment. I knew she was safe. I grabbed two extra clips for my gun, put on my leather jacket and made my way out the door.

CHAPTER XI

"PIECE BY PIECE"

As Nathan regained consciousness and got up off his living room floor after being hit over the head with the lamp. He heard the answering machine, and the voice over the speaker.

"Hi Nathan, it's Gene. Could you please come by the office? I had to stay late. There's a problem with the Morgan file that I think you should see. It's a real important situation, okay? So I hope you get here ASAP, thanks, bye-bye."

Nathan squinted his eyes as he heard the message. His anger was at an all-time high. If there was anything more important to him at this moment, it definitely was revenge. His revenge on Kevin Dawson meant anything that Kevin held close to him was in harm's way.

Nathan made his way to the bathroom and washed his face and scalp. While staring at himself in the mirror, he mumbled, "So that's how you want to play this Mayee. Well, I have something up my sleeve for you and Kevin."

In minutes, Nathan changed his clothes into a Sean John sweatsuit and was ready to begin his mission. On the way to the elevator his phone rang again. He picked up the phone with a hostile attitude. "

Who is it?"

"Nathan it's me, Kurt."

"Do you have Mayee?"

"Yes, she's here."

"Good. Just continue with the plan until I call you. And remember, don't even think about backing out!"

"Nah Man, wouldn't miss this for the world. You're the man, Nathan."

He slammed the phone receiver down on the holder so hard it broke. He grabbed the keys to his Jaguar and went downstairs. On his way through the lobby, he passed the front desk and José snickered and giggled to himself as Nathan passed by. There were three other tenants in the lobby checking their mail while engaged in private conversations on the side. Nathan stopped suddenly and turned to head back toward the front desk.

"Do you find something funny José?"

"Excuse me Mr. Livingston?"

"I said, what the fuck is your homo faggot ass laughing at?"

"I seriously think you need to slow your temper this way! Sssir!"

The other three tenants, two elderly women and one mexican man, turned to see what the commotion was all about.

"What I should do is report your ass to the committee for interfering with the tenants personal affairs" Nathan said loudly.

"Or maybe you should tell them how you paid me $4,000 to give you a blow job 2 years ago? How about that Mr. Woman Beater and Man Eater?"

In the blink of an eye, Nathan snatched José over the counter and began to punch him several times in the face not realizing in that moment that his sudden outburst of fury was validating José's accusations. The tenants in the lobby were screaming for Nathan to release him. Nathan realized a bit too late that he made a big mistake since there were witnesses to this beating. Being a high profile lawyer, he was in more hot water now than he bargained for. Nathan then ran out of the building bumping into a couple on the way to his car. In his rage, Nathan drove through traffic like a mad man all the way to Wall Street. He pulled into the building's underground garage and came to screeching halt. The valet parking attendant was a young black youth who had gotten the job through his parole officer. His probation sentence had been handed down by the same judge Nathan was friends with.

"What's popping' Nathan?"

"Just keep my car close and if I find a scratch on it I'll have your dumb little ass in prison by morning!"

"What?" The young boy replied.

Nathan walked quickly through lobby. The security guards greeted Nathan as he scanned his ID card over the entrance gate. One of the guards tried to give Nathan a message before he got into the elevator. But Nathan waved him off. On his way up to the firm's offices, Nathan balled both of his fists in rage. As he exited the elevator, the night lights gave the office atmosphere a dark gloomy feel. Nathan took a deep breath and made his way through the office checking each cubicle for signs if anyone else stayed behind late. No one was in any of the cubicles. He could see down the hall into the conference room where Gene was sitting twiddling a pencil and scanning the Morgan file. He stood there for a few minutes with a solid statue-like posture. Nathan ran his tongue over the top of his teeth then entered the conference room. Gene was sitting there with a slight smile on her face.

"Thank goodness you're here Nathan. I forgot to get your signature on the last page of the Morgan case. Thank God Judge Barker was on the bench. She gave us a one-day pardon for the document to get signed."

"Are you trying to lose this case Gene?"

"Come on Nathan, it's not that deep. All you have to do..."

"All I have to do is what Gene? Let you ruin the firm by losing one of the most important cases of my career?"

"All I'm saying is..."

"You know what? Maybe I was stupid for even telling Brandon to make you a partner. Or maybe I should let you go and find work at another firm?"

"Nathan, you are talking real crazy!"

"Oh am I? Well then, this is going to sound real crazy – You're fired!"

"Excuse me?"

"Leave the case file on the table and Go home! Get your things tomorrow."

"Oh I get it. You're having a problem keeping your fiancée from being taken from you by my son Kevin, and this is your immature way of dealing with it. So you're going to fire me?"

Nathan and Gene locked eyes for a few seconds. Gene rolled her eyes and began to walk around Nathan. But Nathan's rage was out of control. Nathan grabbed Gene by her throat flinging her onto the table putting his midsection in between Gene's legs as they spread apart. Gene began to struggle gasping for breath.

"You know you're precious little Kevin stepped on the wrong toes and he is going to pay for that."

Nathan smirked at Gene as she gasped for air. She saw the horrifying person being revealed right before her eyes. From out of nowhere, someone grabbed Nathan from behind. He was forcefully pulled off of Gene and thrown to the floor by Brandon.

"Nathan! What the hell are you doing? Are you crazy?"

Brandon carefully helped Gene get up off the conference room table. He turned to Nathan glaring at him with disgust in his eyes.

"I was in the doorway Nathan. I heard everything. How dare you bring this type of behavior into my firm. My father warned me to be careful about you. He also told me about the cover up. That poor young lady. The one you nearly beat to death eight years ago before he passed away. He said it wasn't the cancer that was killing him. It was the guilt. She died Nathan! She died a few days later from internal bleeding and he helped you cover it up. Well, it's been too long Nathan. And if anything happens to me, it's Gene Dawson who gets the billion dollar estate. It's in my father's will. Now get the fuck out of my building. Nathan Livingston, you're fired! Do you hear me!"

Nathan knew he was no match for Brandon. Although scrawny and thin, Brandon was a six-degree black belt in Tai Kwon Do, Jujitsu, and Aikido Kung-Fu. So Nathan put up his middle finger, said fuck you, and left the conference room. On his way down the elevator to the lobby, Nathan pulled his cell phone out and made a call to Kurt who was waiting at the secret location at the South Street Seaport warehouse where Mayee was being held.

"Yes, who's this?" Kurt answered.

"It's me you fucking asshole. Has Kevin shown up yet?"

"Nope!"

"Well where the fuck is he?"

"Ha Ha! I don't know. You're the one running shit, right?"

"Oh, this shit is amusing you?"

"Hell yeah! You're a funny ass dude. But hey you're in control man."

"Whatever. I'm on my way."

"Yesah, I'ze uh be waitin' Massa."

Nathan hung up the phone and then began to pace back and forth in the elevator. When the elevator reached the lobby, the door opened and there was Kevin who had been standing and waiting for the elevator. Kevin grabbed Nathan by his throat and shoved him back into the elevator slamming his back against the wall.

"There's nothing that will stop me from snapping your fucking neck if anything has happened to my mother!"

"Your mother is fine playboy. But Mayee is not going to look as pretty if she's found floating in the Hudson. And you know Kurt better than I do. So let's take a ride."

Kevin released Nathan real slowly while glaring intently into his eyes. His nose hard-pressed close to Nathan's face. Kevin knew Kurt had gone all the way out on this one and wouldn't back out of the deal he made with Nathan. Kevin hit the "open door" button. As the door opened, two security guards were standing there with their hands on their night sticks. They were watching the elevator monitors and had observed what had taken place.

"Wait! It's OK. He's my client and was just a little upset about his case. Everything is fine." Nathan explained to the guards.

As they left the lobby heading to the downstairs garage, Kevin stopped short. "How do I know she's still alive?"

"Well. Let's call your boy and find out." Nathan said with a cynical smile as he dialed Kurt's cell phone.

"Kurt, put Japan Doll on the phone. Your boy wants to say hello."

Nathan passed the phone to Kevin.

"Hello?"

"Kevin, just listen to that mother fucker. And bring his ass here. I got a big surprise for that Nigga!"

"Just put Mayee on the phone Kurt!"

"Hello Kevin. Baby I'm okay. Everything is fine. Just don't do anything until you get here."

"You sure you're okay?" Did Kurt hurt you in anyway?"

"One of his workers tried to rape me in the back room. But Kurt shot him in the head and told me to sit by him until this was all over."

"What!"

Nathan snatched the phone from Kevin quickly then grabbed his wallet and gave the young valet parking attendant a wrinkled $5.00 bill. Kevin punched Nathan in the face knocking him to the ground. He dug in his pocket and gave the kid a $50 bill. The kid laughed at Nathan as he gave him the keys to his Jag.

"You hit me again and you might not make it back at all!"

Kevin already knew that Nathan was going to kill them both. And he would frame Kurt for murders. It was your typical movie cliché for sure. Kevin still had trouble figuring out Kurt's strange behavior. But that was all he had to go on for the moment. Nathan started the car, pulled off and began to head for the pier.

CHAPTER XII

"TIME FOR SOME ACTION"

First, came the thunder. Then the lightning. And then the rain. It began to pour down heavily on Nathan's Jag. It sounded like hundreds of ping pong balls being thrown on the. Nathan was taking his time as he drove up Wall Street heading for the South Street Seaport. He turned on his CD player. Rick James and Tena Marie's duet "Fire and Desire" came blaring out of the speakers. Nathan swayed his head back and forth lip synching to the sound. He didn't make any eye contact for about two minutes into the song. He turned the volume down a few notches. He began tapping his fingers on the steering wheel annoying the shit out of me. All I could do was sit there and look at this piece of shit taunt me with his attitude. All I could do was be quiet...being so fucking fake.

"That was my shit! Damn Kevin! You know, I used to tap Mayee's ass hard to this joint."

"Word? Was that before or after you beat on her?"

"Come on Kevin. Don't act like you never hit your bitch before."

"No! I never hit a bitch before."

"Then some things are never made to perfection Kevin."

"What the fuck are you talking about?"

"You have a minor flaw Kevin. You don't know what's your place is in this world. I bet your father knew his place and he made sure Gene knew hers too."

"Nathan, if you say some shit like that again I'll take both of us out right here...right fucking now."

"Okay, my bad. But now that we have a few moments to spare, let me ask you a question."

"What?"

"Why don't you just let it go? I'm saying, I can't say I didn't underestimate you. But now we both see each other for who we are and what we're obviously up against. Why don't I pull over and we go our separate ways?"

"Our separate ways?"

By the time I realized what he was trying to say, he had pulled the car over to the curb. The rain was still coming down heavy. But I could clearly see the street sign. We were on Allen Street. Somewhere near the fish market. For a minute or two, I sat there and questioned his proposal. I could feel my heart beating again. Faster and faster.

"What the hell are you doing Kevin? Think about this. What's your purpose Kevin?"

I was in love with Mayee and that was that. With nothing else to go on, I remembered years ago when Kurt and I were on 42nd Street coming out of the movie theater. We had just seen one of our favorite all-time action heroes. "Jackie Chan". The movie theater was cheap back then. you could see three movies for $3.50. We had also seen The "Five Deadly Venoms" and "The 18 Bronze Men". It was the two of us having fun Acting like juveniles gone wild.

I remember there were five older dudes two rows behind us who had been getting high. I mean real high. Beer bottles were being thrown around like wrestlers on WWF Smackdown. One of the bottles smashed close to my seat with glass and beer falling over me. I turned to Kurt and began to get up and make my way to the brothers who had thrown the bottle. Kurt stopped me by grabbing my arm. "What the hell are you doing? Those guys are way older than us." My mouth fell open. We used to fight six to seven guys at a time with no fear. I could not understand why all of a sudden he was acting pussy.

Kurt waved me off. Then he Walked over to the group and began to tell them that I was bugging the fuck out, and that I didn't know any better. He sat down in between two of them and began to drink from one of the beer bottles they had smuggled in. They all began to laugh at me while passing Kurt a lit blunt. He was right about one thing. I was bugging the fuck out about seeing that shit.

Kurt yelled down the seats at me "Yo Kevin want some beer?"

"Fuck you nigga!"

"Okay Kevin, I'll just pass this shit back then!"

I smirked and cut my eyes at Kurt.

One of the brothers to Kurt's right told him to pass that shit and he did. (Boosh!) Right over his head. The brother started to scream like a bitch when he saw the blood gushing from his forehead. One down four to go. I followed in a split second jumping over two rows of seats kicking one in the face with my chucks. He was high and it was dark.

At the same time, Kurt elbowed the guy to his left side right in the nose. Three down, two to go. I lost my balance kicking a dude in the face falling forward in between the two brothers who were getting up out of the seats preparing for battle. One of them pulled a fucking sword out of his coat. I mean that knife was huge. He gripped the back handle of the knife and swiped my face like a credit card. Then he grabbed me by the throat and began to choke me while I held his wrist with the knife still pointing directly toward my eye socket. I could hear Kurt still wrestling with the other brother and then the sound of a loud thump. The dude with the knife was pushing harder and harder at my face. I was losing my breath and my strength as I struggled not to get cut again. Kurt came from out of nowhere punching him in his back. The brother let me go and stabbed Kurt right in the stomach. Luckily for Kurt the knife went halfway through the leather bomber and entered only halfway through his upper left side.

As he was holding the guy's wrist, Kurt winked at me and said "Kevin follow my lead and trust me on this one."

Kurt pushed the brother back into the seat where I was still sitting on the floor holding my left cheek. I jumped up behind the dude placed him in a headlock and began to squeeze around his neck. This guy must have been the leader because he was a beast. He started to breathe heavy like a bull. So I squeezed even harder. The dude released his grip on his knife reaching for my arms. Kurt took the knife out of his left side and rammed it right into the guy's chest. All I heard was one short breath and we both dropped in between the seats. It was Kurt's first body. He had killed his first man protecting me.

"Follow my lead. Trust me on this! Follow my lead. Trust me on this!" Rang through my head as I began to snap out of my flashback. I began to laugh out loud. Nathan was staring at me and put a smile on his face. He knew I wasn't going anywhere.

"So I guess that means no?"

"That's right Nathan, you're a pussy!"

"Well then you can give me your gun Kevin. I know you're carrying it. I'm not stupid enough to let you walk in there and get all Chuck Norris."

"Sure Nathan you know you can shoot me now because when it comes down to it, I won't be so passive in return."

I pulled my gun out from behind my back and handed it to Nathan. He searched me again for any hidden weapons. But there were none to be found. He put the gun in his sweats and pulled off into an open gate leading to a warehouse. As he turned a corner I could see two brothers who worked for Kurt on the block guarding the door with guns in their hands. We both got out of the car and walked towards the brothers through the hard rain. When we got to the door it was Lucky and Ant. Two brothers who I was familiar with through Kurt.

Lucky was the first to speak, "Yo Kevin, I'm only following orders man. I think it's fucked up but you know what I'm saying."

Anthony couldn't even look me in the eyes. Anthony used to holler at Kiki when they were in junior high school. She got in between some beef he had with another gang. Anthony was a Blood and, of course, you know Crips are their arch nemesis. It was hard for me to convince both OG heads of the gang that my sister wasn't a member, and her relationship with Ant was over. Because of Ant's beef, three Crips had cornered Kiki and smacked her around. She told Ant about what happened and the war began. Hey, this is what it is.

We entered the warehouse and began to walk through large cases of seafood products. We went through a maze of endless boxes stacked high. We came to a flight of metal stairs and I could see Kurt in the skybox office looking out the window at Nathan and me at the bottom.

Nathan yelled to the top of the stairs, "Mr. Kurt! Bring out that bitch!"

Kurt opened the door, and Mayee walked out first running down the stairs right into my arms. Kurt came down the stairs holding his gun beside his leg. He reached the bottom and stared at me for a few seconds. Nathan grabbed her from my grasp pointing my gun in my face. He took a few steps to the side holding her close to his body. Kurt winked and then smiled at me and I began to laugh loudly.

"How you gonna give that nigga your gun Kevin?" Kurt began to laugh, too.

"How you let that faggot ass get you to do this shit?"

"Yo Kevin, Mayee is a real cool one. I mean, she had me dying up there telling me about her friends. Patricia is my type-A bitch. Ha Ha Ha!"

"Did she tell you about Monica?" I said smiling.

We both started to laugh even harder.

My back was facing the boxes and crates. Nathan and Mayee were standing to my left side about several feet away from my grasp. I was reading Kurt's signals between his words. Suddenly, we heard a noise from behind the boxes. We assumed it had to be Lucky and Anthony coming back to the scene. We were correct. But Lucky had a gun to the back of his head as he walked towards us with his hands held high and Anthony came from behind another box doing the same. Kurt and I had no idea who they were.

"Kurt?" I asked puzzled.

"Kevin be easy." Kurt said turning to Nathan.

"Drop your gun Kurt." Nathan said.

"Fuck you faggot!" Kurt answered.

Nathan glanced quickly at the man holding the gun at Lucky's head. He pulled the trigger splattering Lucky's brains all over the boxes. Nathan looked at the other man the same way.

"Wait a minute man! He's just a little dude!" Kurt yelled at Nathan.

"BLAM! BLAM! He pulled the trigger twice. Spraying little Ant's brains in all directions. I'll never forget Ant's face when he looked at me in the eyes as he slumped to the floor.

"Mother fuckers!" I yelled.

I ran wildly toward Nathan and tackled him to the floor as he kept a tight grip on Mayee while Kurt turned and let off his clip at the two men.

Kurt ran to his left screaming "Come on! Come on!" drawing their fire towards him and away from us on the floor.

Mayee somehow became wedged between Nathan and me as he landed on his back. He pointed his gun directly at my face cocking the hammer back. In the background, I could hear the echoes of gun fire all around us. Moving quickly, I maneuvered her to the side. Somehow, I was able to grab his wrist and point the muzzle of the gun away from my face so that it was slightly to the side of her head. From where she was laying, Mayee screamed out while staring behind me. One of the men was now standing over us pointing his gun at me. I scuffled to gain a hold on Nathan's trigger finger, and was able to release a shot into the man's neck. He grabbed his neck as blood squirted out of the open wound. He managed to get a shot off from his gun grazing Nathan in his shoulder. Nathan screamed and released the gun from his clutch. I pulled her along with me as I rolled off to the side. Mayee was traumatized holding her ears curled up into a ball on the floor. Kurt was behind the boxes reloading his Desert Eagle. The man let off a few shots towards Kurt then he started to run over to where I was holding Mayee. Nathan quickly picked up the gun and grabbed his arm trying to slow down the bleeding. Kurt came from behind the boxes and let off four shots hitting the man in his leg, back and shoulder. Before the man slumped to the floor, he turned around and let off two shots hitting Kurt in the chest. Mayee screamed as Kurt hit the floor. We could hear the police sirens in the far distance. I turned to see where Nathan was. He was gone. I lifted her up off the floor and we both ran over to Kurt. I kneeled down and began to open his shirt.

"You've got to be kidding me Kevin?"

"Chill Kurt, I got you man."

"If you got me, then who's got you?" Kurt said spitting up blood.

"Would you shut the fuck up? I need to see where you got hit" She said to Kurt.

"Hey Kevin, can I ask you a question?"

"Anything Kurt."

"Does her pussy get wet from the excitement?"

All three of us seemed suspended in time. Shaken, I could barely breathe as I lifted his head up while I held his hand. My brother for life. Then Kurt faded out to a place where he could now rest satisfied in a world that would treat him better than this cruel world had. When I finally let go of Kurt, he put his iced-out platinum Jesus chain in my hand.

Then he took his last breath. The high-pitched sounds of police sirens blaring in the night were getting closer.

"We gotta go Kevin." She said with her eyes filled with tears.

"I know, let's get out of here."

We hurried to the back through the boxes and crates. We came to the metal door where Nathan had gone through. The lock was shot off. I opened the door and saw Kurt's Lexus parked by a pier. I told her to run to the car while I went back to get the keys out of Kurt's pocket. I made my way back through the maze of boxes. I saw the lights from their sirens reflecting on the ceiling. I scooted down low and began to go through Kurt's pockets. I found the keys. I decided to take Kurt's wallet for sentimental reasons. I made it back to the Lexus undetected. I pressed the car alarm and started the engine as she jumped in. I drove away with the lights off. I made my way up the back way. Mayee and I scooted down and made a turn on some unknown street. I could see the sign for the way to the FDR. I turned the lights on and peeled off. Out of the blue, Kurt's CD player came on blaring "Mario."

"You should let me love you/let me be the one to/...give you everything you want and need. /Baby good love and protection/ make me your selection/ Show you the way love's supposed to be/...Baby, you should let me love you...love you...love you."

I looked up at the sky through the sun roof. My eyes began to tear. I opened Kurt's wallet and there was an old school picture of me and Kurt at the rooftop skating rink in Harlem. I flipped through some more photographs. There was another picture of Kurt and Kiki posing when Keisha was about 7 years old. Mayee put her hand on my thigh and leaned on my shoulder. All I could do was stare out at the lights as I drove up the FDR and glancing at the water as the moonlit sky smiled down on the waves.

I remembered Kurt's favorite song was Redman's "Time for Some Action."

CHAPTER XIII

"THIS TOO SHALL PASS"

It has been a little over a year since the tombstone was placed over Kurt's grave. Surprisingly the funeral had been packed with old and new faces. Kurt's immediate family was very small. Kurt's half sister Karen, whom I had met once in the past, was married to a music industry A&R who had moved her away from the cold streets of New York City and gave her the love and security Kurt's parents had failed to provide for the two of them. Karen had brought a crew of cousins and close friends from down south areas like Virginia, Atlanta, D.C Maryland and a few from South Carolina towns. Karen had a close, but long distance relationship with her brother. I remember we would talk for hours straight about Kurt and his crazy ass.

Ms. Smith, Kurt's mother, showed up for the wake. She could not stay long because she was in another drug rehab facility that would not allow her to stay through the whole service. She looked exceptionally healthy and gained a lot of her weight back. I believe that was the longest time that Ms. Smith had stayed clean from crack. I believe she lost her son when she was using. And losing him for a second and final time, it helped her find the strength to want to change her life for the better.

It took me several months to get my credit back to normal. Nathan had really screwed me up. Theresa had some problems too. It seems the both of us got under Mr. Livingston's skin the most. My mother Gene made partner immediately after her encounter that night with Nathan and Brandon. She attended therapy sessions for almost six months. Paid for by Brandon and the firm.

My sister decided to go to college. She grew real close to Mayee, Theresa, Patricia and Monica during the year. It got to the point where whenever there was a gathering among us, Kiki was sure to be there. They took her under their wings, and gave her sisterly guidance. She was accepted to New York University with the help from them all. She was also ready to pledge Delta Sigma Theta.

Nathan was forced to sell his condo in midtown. For a while, he remained the front-page news story when it was discovered that he was no longer a partner at Teller, and was also being sued by a gay man named José, for assault and civil rights violations. Nathan was never actually found guilty but gave José an out-of-court settlement for $300,000. It was rumored that he bought a house in New Jersey and simply dropped out of sight.

Because of Kurt's police record and history of involvement with street crimes, his death at South Street Seaport was officially filed "case closed – drug related."

For the past year, Mayee and I have been side by side. Just like Neo and Trinity from the movie I love the most "The Matrix". We bought guns, took martial arts lessons during our spare time, and wore all black leather suits topped off with Christian Dior sunglasses. Call it what you want. But after knowing what Nathan was capable of doing, we were taking no chances.

Maybe Nathan was just playing the waiting game while we all took a breather for the smoke to clear. Or maybe he was over Mayee. And had come to his senses and moved on. No one was certain about everything that happened or how it would it all end up. The only certainty is that life must continue.

Today is a real important day for me. Sunzu, Mayee's mother has been invited over for dinner. She has avoided meeting me for the past year. Although I have been over to their house a couple of times to pick her up, I would try to start small conversations with Sunzu. She always acted as though she was evading me.

The time was 7:00 p.m. and Mayee was in the bedroom talking on the phone with her mother confirming her dinner arrangement with us for the evening. She was sitting on my bed in a yoga position wearing only a thong and bra. I had taken a break from prepping the kitchen before cooking my special meal for her mom. I walked to the bedroom door and stared at her as she continued talking on the phone. Even though we were dining indoors, Mayee still had a beautiful black evening gown spread across the bed. Seeing her half naked was making me horny and I felt the passion rise in me. I still could not believe after a year of sexing her, it still felt like our first two weeks together all over again. No matter how many crazy positions I would bend her up in, her pussy never seemed to stretch or feel worn out.

As she was talking I walked over to her and gently pushed her back on the bed. Her legs were spread wide open. She smiled and continued to talk to her mother. I took my finger and pulled her thong to the side and began to eat her out. She covered her eyes with her free hand and bit her bottom lip as I ran my tongue on the walls of her vagina. I extended my arms reaching up to her breasts and began to fondle her nipples. She giggled and told her mother she would call her back in a few minutes and hung up the phone.

I stopped licking her and began to stand up when she stopped me and scooted to the edge of the bed. Her face was leveled directly in front of my dick. She pulled my boxers down to my ankles, took hold and began to slowly do me in the same way. She was sucking me real gently and slow. It was definitely feeling very good, but it is the little things that turn me on.

When her hair was out, she would continue to give me head while at the same time putting her hair up in a bun. Every time I saw her do that it brought me closer to climax. This time I think she realized it by the way my dick jerked in her mouth. So she looked up at me, took her hair out and repeated the same motion. She also sucked me harder and faster.

She had never let me cum in her mouth before. She thought it was nasty. This time she let me go all the way. After I had released in her mouth, she pushed me back very slow, closed her eyes really tight and swallowed.

She looked up at me and I could tell she was uncomfortable with what she had just done. So I broke the ice by singing Notorious BIG, "I love it when ya call me Big Papa...throw your hands in the air, if you'ze a true player."

"Don't even feel yourself nigga." She said slapping my dick.

"Oowww. Are you crazy?"

She wrestled me to the floor and sat on my stomach as I started to laugh. She pinned both my arms to the floor bending forward with her face in front of mine. As I was laughing, she stuck her tongue in my mouth. Her breath smelled like semen. I pushed her face away with my cheek.

"What's the matter Kevin? You can't kiss me now? She said with a smile.

"Hell No!"

"Oh it's like that now?"

"Hell yeah!" I smiled.

"Fuck you Kevin!" she said getting up off my stomach. She stood over me fixing her thong and looked down smiling at me. "Pussy breath Kevin."

"Cum breath. Go brush your teeth."

She began to laugh as she made her way out of the room to go brush her teeth. I lay on the floor for a few minutes gathering my thoughts. I began to brush my hand over the carpet enjoying the softness when I noticed a shoebox under my bed. It was a box for some Timberlands, but what caught my attention was the size? I wear a size 12, but these were size 9 1/2.

I jumped up off the floor and moved backwards out of the room slowly. My bathroom is next door to my bedroom. I had a serious expression of fear on my face. Mayee was standing at the bathroom sink gargling some mouthwash when she noticed my movements. She spat the mouthwash out into the sink and turned to me.

"What's wrong Kevin?"

"There's a shoe box under my bed?"

"So why are you looking crazed?"

"It's not my size."

We both stood there very still and quiet for about 10 seconds then we yelled at each other.

"BOMB!"

She dashed right past me heading towards the living room. I followed behind her as fast as I could. I somehow bumped into her back making her fall completely over the sofa. She grabbed some throw pillows on her way down tossing them up in the air. One of them hit me dead center in my face blocking my view causing my knee to smash hard into the living room table. I fell to the floor landing beside her.

She grabbed my arm to help me get up screaming, "Come on man," but my knee was in so much pain that I kept stumbling all over her making her lose her balance. After we managed to get ourselves together, I put my arm over her shoulder and we hauled ass towards the front door. I was hopping all over the place like a Three-legged dog. She tried to unlock the door, but couldn't figure out how. I began to shout at her.

"Turn that shit bitch!"

"I'm trying nigga!"

"Pull the mother fucker and wiggle it!"

"I'm trying to Kevin. but it won't come out."

"Let me try."

"You can't because you're all bent over."

"Pull it Mayee!"

"Stop pushing so hard Kevin!"

When we finally got the door open we ran out the door into the hall with her dressed only in her thong and bra, and me wearing only my boxers. We ran dead smack into her mother... Sunzu. She had been listening to the entire crazy drama from the other side of the door. I can only imagine what she thought Mayee and I had been doing in my apartment.

"Mom?"

"Ms. Sunzu?"

"And this is what you wanted me to see?"

"No Mom, I can explain."

"Well, I'm waiting?"

"Umm...well see...umm...there's a...umm."

I told her to stay there with her mother while I went back into the apartment to check the box. Sunzu took her coat off and gave it to Mayee to cover herself. I made my way back to my bed took a deep breath and reached for the box. I pulled it from under the bed slowly and placed it on the bed. The box had some weight to it making me extra paranoid about opening the lid. I remembered vacuuming my carpet and leaving shoeboxes untouched was a common thing for me. Mayee and Sunzu were standing in the doorway staring at me while I lifted the box lid slowly. My eyes widened when I saw what was in the box. It was at least $200,000 in cash with an envelope on top.

Sunzu shook her head and said she would be in the living room still waiting to hear our explanations for what she had witnessed. As she walked away, she began to laugh to herself. Hearing her chuckle to herself made the whole scene seem funny. Mayee covered her mouth and sat down beside me. I then remembered that Kurt was a size 9 1/2. He must have placed it there that night. I had a general idea of what the letter might contain. He must have known something was going to go wrong and this was his way of setting straight what he had done.

I told her that some things are just personal and I wanted to read the letter in privacy and whatever was written was for my eyes only. She grabbed her evening dress, kissed my forehead and went into the bathroom to get dressed. She closed the door on her way out.

I did not read the letter. I placed it back in the box and put it in my closet for later. I took out one of my most expensive suits and a pair of Giorgio's then I got dressed and went straight to the kitchen. I was totally embarrassed and couldn't face Sunzu just yet.

Mayee and Sunzu sat on the couch talking as if nothing had occurred. I could not quite hear them but it sounded like they were whispering about something. I was in the middle of prepping some green peppers when I was startled by Sunzu standing behind me.

"Move over young man."

She rolled up her sleeves and took the knife out of my hand. She smiled looking just as beautiful as her daughter. From the kitchen I could see Mayee giggling out on the couch.

"I heard about you being a fancy chef, but I'll show you some real ancient Japanese secrets." Sunzu said pushing me aside. "And can you please put on some Jay-Z? I like listening to my homeboy while I cook."

Chapter XIV

"New Beginnings"

After I had watched Mayee's mother cook us a fabulous Asian meal from scratch, I found myself truly appreciating the beauty of her culture. The meal was like nothing I had ever tasted from dining out at Japanese restaurants. I truly believe that Asians will never show American chefs all of their real recipes to recherché menus that are handed to us.

I placed the dishes carefully into the dishwasher. The set was a rare porcelain Japanese set that my grandmother had given to me for a housewarming gift. Sunzu had complimented my granny's taste after the meal. Mayee and Sunzu were looking at my family photo album when I entered the living room. Sunzu didn't seem to be paying any attention because she was staring at me with a curious look on her face. I played it off as if I hadn't noticed her staring and walked over to the lamp by the wall unit. I really did not have a reason to be over there, so I just pretended to dim the lights to set the mood for a comfortable conversation.

Mayee was trying to tell her about how wonderful my younger sister Keisha. But her mother was more focused on my movements. I sat down next to Mayee trying not to touch her in any way that might appear inappropriate for the setting. I was already embarrassed by Sunzu seeing me and Mayee partially naked. Being that it was Sunzu's first time over to visit since Mayee and I had become a couple. I guess Mayee was feeling the vibes bouncing between me and her mother so she closed the book. She put her hair in a ponytail and began to prepare for the conversation she knew her mother was waiting for.

"So Mom, I know you're concerned about where this is going and what me and Kevin plan to do in the future with our relationship."

"Of course I'm concerned Mayee. I'm not denying the fact that you both are in love. But there are other factors to consider here."

"Like what mom? And please don't bring up the fact that interracial relationships don't work out."

"All I'm saying is you and Kevin may need to look at this in a realistic way. How does his family feel? How do I feel? You're not just in a relationship together your whole family is involved too. And what about your children?"

"Ms. Sunzu, my family accepts any decision I make for myself. I'm a grown man and Mayee is a grown woman and together we make adult decisions."

Sunzu folded her arms and leaned back into the corner of the couch. Her face went cold as she stared at me and Mayee avoiding direct eye contact with her daughter. Did I offend her? Had I been over-assertive with my reply? I knew it was about to get ugly for me in about 10 seconds.

"Let me tell you about adult decisions and not thinking before you speak." Sunzu said pointing her finger at me and Mayee.

"When I met Mayee's father, he was in the Marines and stationed at the U.S. embassy in Japan. I was working there as a full-time catering tabletop. My mother was a file clerk and my father could not stand us both working there. But my mother told me one day that things would change and get better for me. I would soon have to make a choice and decide what was best for me and the child that was growing inside me. I was so terrified to tell my mother that the baby's father was not only an American, but an African-American. I gave birth to Mayee hoping her features wouldn't show any traces of her father's ethnic background."

Mayee had never heard her mother tell this story before. So she sat there with her eyes beginning to water as Sunzu continued.

"When my father realized that Mayee was mixed, his rage was uncontrollable. He began to throw all the hospital equipment around injuring the doctors and my mother in the process. He was so upset that he began to scream at my mother as she laid on the floor saying it was her fault for what had happened, and she had known about the pregnancy. My mother begged him to believe that she had no idea about what was going on. He believed her but was still outraged. He disowned me that day. I married Mayee's father in order to get a U.S. citizenship. I then moved here in order to give Mayee a better life. But, at what cost? I lost my family."

Sunzu said she had to use the bathroom, got up and left the both of us sitting there stunned. I hugged Mayee real tight while tears ran down her face. I was speechless. I did not know what to say to her after hearing how her mother had been tragically affected by being in an interracial relationship. We could only sit there in silence curled up next to each other.

Sunzu returned from the bathroom. Before sitting back down, she sat between us, grabbed both of our hands, and smiled.

"I want you both to know that I have been paying close attention to the both of you. I give to you Kevin, my daughter Mayee in order to honor my family tradition."

"Mom we don't have a family tradition." Mayee said smiling.

"Well we do now. And if Kevin doesn't fulfill his obligation to his new family, I'll hire a government assassin to kill him."

"What?" I said, letting go of Sunzu's hand.

Sunzu began to laugh so hard that Mayee had to wonder if her mother was drunk from the wine. I chuckled nervously at first, and started to laugh along with Sunzu. She pulled me close and gave me a hug and she told Mayee that I was so cute and handsome she was lucky to have a man like me who was willing to protect her as I did. We continued to enjoy the rest of the evening exchanging family stories.

When it was time for Sunzu to go home, I helped her put her coat on and walked her to the door. She gave me a kiss on my cheek, waved goodbye to Mayee, and told me I was also welcomed to her house any time. I asked her if she wanted me to walk her down to her car, but she declined and left my house smiling.

I walked back into the living room while Mayee was putting a CD in the player. She put a Black Street jam in the carousel, selected a song appropriate for the mood. "Let's Stay in Love," and we started to slow dance holding each other real close.

"Kevin?"

"What's up baby?"

"How do you feel about kids?"

"I think they're noisy, messy and do nothing but cry and beg for toys. When they shit they stink up the whole place."

"Kevin!"

"I'm just playing. I like kids. Why?"

"How do you feel about being a father?"

"Are you saying?"

"I'm not sure yet. I haven't had my period in almost two months now."

I continued holding her close but said nothing to her for a few seconds.

"Well nigga say something!"

"Okay, How about we go down to the 24-hour store and pick up one of those First Response pregnancy tests?"

"I'm scared Kevin."

"You're scared? Now you're all about being a punk."

"I ain't no punk! Bitch!" She said pushing me back.

"So let's go then, punk!"

"Fuck you Kevin! Let's go then!"

"Fine!"

"Fine then!"

We laughed at each other as we put on our coats to go down to the store. I couldn't help smiling because I haven't really thought about kids. I was still scared for her not knowing what rock Nathan would crawl from under in the future. If he even came back some day. We both hugged each other and waited for the elevator holding hands. When we got down to the lobby, I ran into one of my ex-girlfriends going to visit a friend who lived in my building. Her name was Sandra, but I called her Sandy.

"Oh shit! Kevin Dawson!"

"Hey Sandy, how are you girl?"

"I'm chillin' Boo."

I thought that her calling me Boo would get Mayee up set. But Mayee was a handful of maturity. She smiled and told me to take my time and that she'll be in front waiting. She also said hi to Sandy on the way out.

"What's up with the takeout order girl?"

"Sandy, watch yourself. You know I never let anyone disrespect you. so show some respect."

"Okay Kevin. I know how sensitive you are about your women. I'm cool."

"Anyway Sandy, how's your mom?"

"She passed away last year from cancer."

"I'm sorry to hear that. She was real cool."

"Please...All she kept saying for about a year after we broke up was, what happened to that fine ass Kevin? She really liked you too."

"So what's up with Cheryl?

"She's moved down south to ATL with two kids."

"Damn Sandy! She was loose as hell. Who married her crazy ass?"

"Anyway, Kevin what about you?"

I had to think for a few seconds before answering. Did I want to put all that had happened out on Front Street? I knew Sandy would tell the world. Through the glass window in the lobby, I could see Mayee standing impatiently outside. She looked so cool and sexy and calm.

I said to myself. Fuck it.

"I think I'm about to be a father soon. We're on our way to get the pregnancy test."

"What?!" Sandy said loudly. Mayee heard her through the glass making her look inside.

"What's her name Kevin?"

"Mayee. Why?"

"Excuse me Mayee, can you come in here girl?" Sandy said loudly enough for her to come back into the lobby. Mayee's face expression was still calm as ever as she walked over to us.

"Congratulations, girl! Kevin told me you and he are expecting a baby."

"Ummm...I'm not sure yet, but thank you," "thank you for slowing his ass down. Oh my God, Kevin was crazy loose. What about Kurt?" Sandy asked.

I put my head down looking at the floor and began to bite my bottom lip. She knew what that meant.

"Oh my God Kevin, I'm sorry."

"It's okay Sandy. He's really loose now up in heaven driving God crazy."

We all stood there for a moment of silence for Kurt.

"Well my name is Sandra. And it was a pleasure to meet you Mayee."

"It was a pleasure for me too."

"Well Sandy my number is still the same. Call if you wanna holla."

"I also own my own party supplies store. So when you have that baby shower Mayee, everything is free for you and my Boy, okay?"

Sandy waved goodbye and entered the elevator. Mayee smiled and grabbed my hand pulling me out through the exit door. Walking down the block arms locked it began to lightly snow. I could not believe it was December and Christmas was right around the corner. So much had happened I guess we lost track of time. We were so in love it almost seemed to be a dream.

We entered the 24-hour Rite Aid store on 72nd Street. The store was packed with people getting Christmas supplies and catching the sales for the holidays. We both walked up to the counter and asked the cashier where we could find the pregnancy test. The cashier pointed to Row 4. She giggled like a little girl as she continued to pull me around like a rag doll.

While we were comparing prices, I noticed a familiar face staring at us from afar. I could not put my finger on where I knew him. He walked towards us and lightly brushed against my jacket as he headed down the aisle. She was kneeling down looking at the boxes while I stood over her back. I continued to stare at the brother's back as he turned slightly, only revealing his profile.

"Mayee! Get up! Let's go!"

"What's wrong Kevin?"

"That guy who just left the store."

She jumped up quickly dropping the boxes from her hand on the floor. I grabbed her hand and we rushed to the front of the aisle. I pushed her behind me and peeked around the toilet paper that was stacked at the entrance.

"Is there a problem, sir?" A voice suddenly came from behind us startling Mayee making her jump. I grabbed the manager by his shirt not thinking. Just reacting, he screamed like a little girl. So I let him go slowly.

"I think someone is following my wife around. I'm sorry." I said smiling.

"Do you want me to call the police?" The manager said holding his chest.

"No, I think he's left the store." She said looking at me shrugging her shoulders.

"I think I'm going to have to ask for y'all to leave sir."

"No problem. We don't want any problems," I said while flashing a couple of hundred dollar bills. She smacked me in the back of my head.

"Why do you always do that shit?! It ain't cute Kevin."

We left the store and were standing outside looking up and down the street. But there was no sign of the mystery man. We began to walk back to my place when a car began following us. First Mayee noticed. Then I looked over her shoulder to see what she was looking at. As the car continued to follow us it pulled up ahead and stopped at the corner. The door opened slowly. And Nathan Livingston stepped out.

CHAPTER XV

"EVERY BEGINNING"

I pushed Mayee back behind me and played my position. She moved from behind me and began throwing her hands in the air screaming at Nathan as he walked towards us.

"What the fuck do you want from me?! What the fuck is your problem! You wanna keep this shit going mother fucker? Come on then!"

"Mayee! Get behind me!" I shouted out.

"No! This ain't about you Kevin! This is about me and him! We gonna end this shit right now! I'm not running away another fucking day from you Nathan! So what's it gonna be?"

Nathan put his hands up and showed us that his hands were empty. Then he turned around doing a 360 while lifting his coat up and showed his waist. He was not carrying any weapons.

"So, where's your hit men Nathan?" I said looking up and down the street.

"I don't know what you're talking about? I came alone. I swear it. I'm alone. I know this is not what you were expecting. I'm a changed man. I came to make amends to the people I've hurt the most. I need to do this for myself. I've been in therapy for almost a year now. I have not told anyone in my groups what happened between us, but please give me a chance or at least..."

Nathan stopped talking and grabbed his face with both palms. We could hear him mumble to himself,

"I knew this wasn't a good idea."

Then he began to walk back to his car. Mayee sucked her teeth and started screaming at Nathan again.

"No! It's not going to be that easy for you Nathan! Let's hear the bullshit. Tell us how you've changed Nathan. Tell us how your miracle healing is going to bring back a life you took."

Nathan froze with his back facing us. She moved away from him bringing a crowd around us. I pulled her by her coat and told her to slow down and to remember that we could be charged with withholding information from a homicide investigation.

She screamed, "No!" then placed her face into the center of my jacket and began to cry. Nathan turned to us and begged us to talk about what had happened. But somewhere else.

"Well, where are we going to go Nathan?" I asked him sarcastically.

"I have a spot that I go to that's public and has a soothing setting. I have no tricks up my sleeve and I don't intend to harm anyone anymore."

"You expect us to get in your car? I think you know better Nathan."

"I understand. So can you meet me there in an hour?"

"Where is this spot Nathan?"

"It's Rockefeller Center. We can sit by the Christmas tree. There are a lot of people around so you and Mayee can feel safe."

"I don't know if Mayee wants to..."

"It's okay Kevin. Let's get this over with. We'll be there! Let's go Kevin."

She walked away crossing her arms and sucking her teeth. I looked at Nathan and backed away turning around to catch up with her.

Then Nathan called to me, "Kevin! I have something that belongs to you. I would appreciate it if you would take this off my hands."

I knew he was talking about the gun I had dropped in the warehouse at South Street Seaport. I still wasn't sure what was going on, but I knew if I had the gun back I could get rid of it. And it was better for me to do it than leave it in someone else's possession. I walked back to his car. He handed me a brown paper bag with the gun in it.

I had to be sure Nathan wasn't pulling a stunt, so I leaned in the car window and told Nathan to be straight up and let me know what he was really trying to do. He looked me dead in the eyes and told me he was trying to clean his soul...Finally. He wasn't lying. I could see what appeared to be sincerity in his eyes. I nodded my head and ran up the street back to her. I finally caught up to her standing at a light pole waiting for me to come back. We began to walk back to my house but the keys to my Caddy were on my key chain. So we went straight to the truck. I pressed the alarm on the key chain opening the automatic doors. She was real quiet getting inside the truck. We both sat there while heat from the vents began to warm us up. I put the brown paper bag on the floor between my feet pushing it under the seat.

"What's that Kevin?"

"It's my gun."

"I don't trust Nathan Kevin. I think you should get rid of it now!"

"But what if it's a trap?"

"I love you Kevin. But all of this Matrix shit has got to stop. In fact, as soon as we get back, all of the other guns have got to go too!"

"Now you're bugging the fuck out!"

"Kevin!" She hollered.

"I'm saying though..."

"Kevin, I'm about to have a fucking baby alright! I'm not a violent person. So if you want to keep violence around you, then fine. But I will leave you Kevin. I've seen enough violent shit already."

"Okay! Fine!" I shouted.

"Fine then!" She shouted back.

"Fine!" I yelled back.

We both sat there staring in opposite direction out the windows. I turned back after a few seconds.

"Do you mean fine you're leaving? or do you mean fine you believe me?"

She slapped me in the back of my head and began to laugh out loud. She grabbed my cheeks and kissed me.

"You're so cute Kevin. Of course I believe you."

We pulled off and headed towards Rockefeller Center to meet Nathan. She strongly suggested that I get rid of the gun. So I made a detour and drove to the West Side Highway. When we reached the Hudson River, I threw the gun into the waters as far as I could. Then I jumped back into the truck rolling my eyes at her as I pulled off. We finally arrived at Rockefeller Center. I found a parking space and we made our way to the area where Nathan said he wanted to meet us. We didn't see Nathan, so we sat down and watched the tree trimming while we waited for him to show up. It was amazing how they find their way up this tree that stands 50 ft to 60 ft. high. We sat there in amazement for about 30 minutes. We heard Nathan call out to us through the crowd. In his hands he held three cups of Starbuck's coffee sitting in a cardboard holder. I reached for one of the cups but Mayee slapped my hand down away from the cup.

"What is it that you have to say to us Nathan?" Mayee asked pissed off.

"I want you to walk with me awhile. So I can tell you both about my childhood. I just want you to listen. And then you can go and never see me again."

Mayee and I were getting the picture. Nathan was coming out of his closet. We knew and had heard that "cleaning out your closet" meant going back to your past and facing your demons. A therapist would have you relive your pain in order to move on. She grabbed a cup of coffee. So I followed and did the same. I mumbled under my breath that I was getting cold and the shit was free anyway. We began to walk and Nathan began to spilling.

"First off, I can't take back what I've done. There is no money or anything I can give you Kevin to bring Kurt back or my ex-girlfriend. I know this might sound cold, but, I'm not turning myself in. If anyone understands, it should be you Kevin. We do what we do as human beings, but we are all weak in the flesh as Christians would say. I pray for forgiveness every night until the Lord feels my punishment should be handed down to me."

We found ourselves walking down one of those one-way streets as Nathan continued to talk. She stayed close by my side listening intently as I was.

"My father was a cold-hearted man. His idea of power was controlling his family's destiny. And violently too. He would do all kinds of crazy shit to me and my mother to show he was the king of his household. It started when I was 7 years old. If my report card had anything less than an "A" average, he would tie me and my mother up to a pole in the basement and beat us until one of us passed out. He would say we had to be disciplined and know our place in the world. Although I never drank alcohol, he did on a regular basis. So he would abuse us regularly. I hope you are both getting the message. I can't talk with so much pain and confusion in my head right now."

Mayee told Nathan to slow down and not to get all worked up. We all took sips from our cups and walked real slow down a quiet street.

"Wow Nathan I'm fucked up too about my pops, but I guess someone always teaches us to count our blessings." I said quietly.

"Nathan, you really hurt me. And it would be hard for me to say I understand. But you've been the victim too. I hope you find the peace you're looking for and I wish you a good recovery." She said holding my arm close to her.

"So I guess I'll just say it. I'm sorry for what I've done to hurt you both. And I'm happy you found someone who will treat you right Mayee."

Nathan extended his hand to me hoping I would shake it. A gesture of agreeing to the peace between us as men. I started to shake his hand, when I noticed the same man from the Rite Aid store crossing the street approaching us with his hands in his pockets.

"What the fuck is this Nathan? A Goddamn set up?"

"What are you talking about Kevin?"

Nathan said looking stunned as the man approached closer. Mayee grabbed my jacket pulling me away. The man stopped right in front of Nathan and me.

"I don't know this man?"

Nathan said still looking surprised.

Mayee and I paused for a second. She pointed at the man. I pointed also.

"I remember you!" Mayee said surprised.

"Yeah, I remember you too!"

I said still pointing at the man.

"Well I don't know him."

Nathan said shrugging his shoulders.

He was the brother who was at the Club the same night I met Mayee. He'd been sitting at the bar talking to that young lady when I had squeezed myself in between them to talk to her. The same brother with the stitched up lip who I thought looked cooler than Denzel Washington.

CHAPTER XVI

"HAS AN ENDING"

I still couldn't figure out what was going on with this scenario. What was the brother doing following us around? How long had he been following us? What was his purpose in this crazy equation? We all stood there staring at each other. Somebody had to say something.

"So is there a reason why you've been following me homeboy?" I asked backing up again clutching my fist.

"I wasn't following you. It's all about the Girl." the man answered.

"What the fuck did you say?"

I stepped up real close to his face.

For some reason the street was now eerily vacant and quiet. No one but the four of us was standing there. Then he pulled out a gun and pointed at my face. I turned around looking at her and scrunched up my lips at her.

"You see! Get rid of the gun huh!" I said sarcastically.

"My problems not with you Kevin!" He said and pointed the gun at Nathan.

"How do you know my name?" I asked.

"You see it's like this Kevin. I had to follow your girl here in order to get close to Nathan Livingston. I knew she was his girl at the time. I was waiting for the right time to make my move on this piece of shit. Then you stepped into the picture. I've been waiting 10 years for my chance to kill him. But things got interesting when I got the call from a mutual friend of ours."

"Are you talking about Kurt?"

"Yes Kurt. He took me in when I was a little dude who had been lost and left to the streets."

"What does any of this have to do with me?" Nathan asked nervously.

The man smacked Nathan in the face with the gun knocking him to the ground. He then he stood over him with the barrel of his gun pointed at the back of Nathan's head. I leaped back and asked the man to be cool about what was about to go down. He stared at me like I was crazy.

"I know Nathan is a piece of shit. And probably deserves to die. But why are you doing this shit in front of me?"

"Well, I see the great Kevin has gone soft for love and come out on top -- but what about me? I lost my only love because of Nathan. And now he's gonna pay for his crime. Yeah, the lawyer of the year – serving justice was your job Nathan. But you used your power to kill and escape."

"Who are you? And what did I do to you man?" Nathan pleaded while keeping his eyes tightly closed.

"What did he do?"

She asked trembling.

"The same thing he did to you! He abused and beat my sister! Do you remember me now Nathan? You smacked me in the mouth with your shoe when I was 9 years old. You were beating my sister and I tried to stop you! She was all I had to live for. You called her a crackhead. You know she never used drugs especially after my mother had died from an overdose. But you beat her until she lapsed into a coma! She died three days later. And you covered it up. I was left to survive on the streets alone with no one. The police asked me about you because your DNA was found inside her after you had fucked her like a dog. Even while she was unconscious you still got on top of her and fucked her!"

We each realized he was just a teenager about 19 years old. And was still a baby. In that moment my mind became a jumble of thoughts and it seemed that my life was flashing before me. Childhood memories of my own family household. All the nights on 42nd Street snatching chains, robbing white folks for their wallets and purses, learning about pimping from the OGs. Having my first sexual experience with a street prostitute. Learning how to smoke weed and drink alcohol. Moving up in the game from selling weed to selling cocaine. Learning how to make a profit. Not using. And fighting anyone who opposed me or my right hand man Kurt. I could see me through this young brother like an early image of myself.

Everything came flooding back: club hopping at Studio 54, the Palladium, The Limelight, Club S&S, the Disco Fever, the Rooftop. Watching the birth of Hip-Hop. Bronx River Street battles. Africa Bambaataa, the Zulu nation, Dougie Fresh & Slick Rick, Cold crush brothers. Melly Mel and the Furious 5. Busy Bee Starski, The Treacherous Three, AJ-Les. The 70's-80's was my time. The 90s and the world as we know it, now had been a reflection of what we had created. The youth have a new way. But we are molded by the real street pioneers. I felt responsible as a black man who may have showed the youth the direction to destruction. We are the teachers. If I had shown that it's okay to beat a women, rob and steal, carry guns, and kill with no compassion about life, then how can I expect the generations that follows to learn a different way?

I pushed Mayee gently to the side. I began to take the chain off my neck that belonged to Kurt and held it up in front of the young man as he held the gun to Nathan's head.

"What's that gonna do Kevin? Keep me from blowing his brains out?" He asked without blinking an eye.

"Can you give us a name first?" I asked.

"Come on Kevin, you should know who I am? It was you who told me when I was 8 years old to always be a man and never let my enemies live. It was you who was my sister's favorite first boyfriend. You were the only one who would take time to play with me. I remember how you would buy me Mr. Softy ice cream cones."

I remembered who his sister was. I had been in high school at the time. Barely passing my classes because I would be so tired from hanging and banging. I would ask a girl named Sharon to do my homework for me. Sharon had fallen in love with me. I would go to her block and hang out with her hoping to get some ass. But she told me she was a virgin. And I was no rapist. So I would just buy her little gifts.

"Jay? Little Jay?"

"That's correct Kevin. I was peeking through the door when Sharon asked you to stop. You told her you were sorry for trying to pressure her into having sex. And I remembered how happy she was after that. You gave her $200 and told her to go buy me some toys. But you never came back. And even though she was heartbroken, she would talk about you everyday, telling her friends how special you treated girls. She always told me to be like you."

Jay cocked the hammer back on the gun. Nathan looked up at me and Mayee with this look in his eyes. As if he had a moment of clarity. Then He smiled. And Jay pulled the trigger... A splatter of blood hit me as Nathan went down. I closed my eyes when I heard the blast. I believed that Nathan's judgment day had finally arrived. Mayee didn't even scream. She was speechless. As she stood there in complete shock. I finally opened my eyes and I could see Nathan's skull and brain fragments on the sidewalk while Jay just stared at me and her. His face was so cold. So absent of any emotional attachment whatsoever. I blinked slowly as I released the chain from my hand listening to it clatter against the concrete on impact. Jay walked over to the chain and picked it up. He placed it around his neck letting it rest on his chest.

"Now I'll ask the Lord for forgiveness! Now that there's justice. And I shall be judged. As I judged him for his sins. Your pain Mayee, is now my burden to carry. Now take Japanese Doll and get out of here."

I watched Jay with sorrow in my eyes. Mayee said nothing. She just pulled my jacket, and I followed. As we hurried up the empty street trying to get back to Rockefeller Center hoping to fade into the crowd, I looked back one last time. I saw Jay still standing over Nathan's lifeless body. I turned away and looked into the crowd watching people laugh together in small groups. I could not believe that no one was aware of what had happened just 3 to 4 blocks away from the festivities. When she glanced back down the street, Jay seemed to have vanished in thin air.

"Kevin?" She asked pulling my jacket.

"What?" I answered blowing heat into my hands with my breath.

"I feel sick Kevin. I wanna sit down."

"It's okay Mayee. It's over now."

I began to cuddle her trying to warm her shivering body with some heat. All of a sudden, a voice came through the crowd. We each looked around to see who was calling out my name?

It was Jay standing a few feet away in the crowd with a cup of coffee in his hand. A small group of Japanese tourists passed alongside making his body appear to fade in and out of the crowd. When he came into view, he shouted,

"I forgot to tell you... Merry Christmas! I left you a present under your bed. There's a letter I think you should read with Japanese Doll."

Then in seconds, he was gone again. One of the Japanese tourists, a man, approached Mayee speaking in Japanese causing her to smile at me as she got up. I sat there as the man handed her a camcorder video still speaking in Japanese, as the group crowded together in front of the huge tree. She began to record them as she spoke Japanese herself. This was the first time I heard her speak her language. The ambulance sirens approached closer as she continued to talk Japanese and film the group.

She took a second to look away from the camera to watch my response. I gave her a thumbs up and whispered to her not to panic as we were well in the clear. Several police cars zoomed up the same street where I'm sure Nathan's dead body had been discovered. Mayee bowed to the group of tourists and made her way back to sit down beside me. We watched the Channel 7 news truck zoom up the same street behind the police cars.

Then irony revealed itself plain as day. We could hear people in the distance spreading the news like a bad joke. "Nathan Livingston the lawyer was shot dead up the street!"

Most of the people were tourists. So no one was curious. No one cared. No one moved but a few city residents ran to view the crime scene.

"Kevin I need to ask you a question."

"Anything you want."

"How many people have you killed?"

"None!"

I answered while looking away from her eyes with a serious expression pasted on my face. She grabbed my face and looked into my eyes again seeing right through to my soul.

"You don't have to tell me anything you don't want to Kevin. I'm in love with you. And I know about secrets now. You have a power Kevin. A gift that is greater than you know. You have a purpose for me. You opened up doors for me to learn what's out there. You gave me sight. I believe you've done more good than harm in your life. And if you could show one person how to live the right way, I'm sure it will be our baby. Your child will know how to help others. And give the gift back."

"Thank you Mayee. I love you too."

I took her hand and walked back to my truck.

CHAPTER XXVII

"THE LETTER"

Pulling up in front of my building, I noticed that there was a parking space dead center in front of the entrance. I told Mayee there's never been a space that close to my building before. She smiled at me as she grabbed her stuff off the back seat. I turned the truck off and began to open the door when we were startled by a knock on the window. It was Kiki, Patricia, Monica and Theresa standing outside of the truck. They were parked a few cars behind my truck when they saw us pull up. I rolled down the window. Keisha was shaking her head.

"Yo Kevin, you heard about Nathan?"

"Yeah Kiki, that's fucked up."

"Come on Bro, it's cold out here."

Patricia, Monica, and Theresa started walking ahead to the building. She stared at them through the windshield as she got out of the truck.

"Mayee, do you mind if I talk to my brother alone for a few?"

"No problem." She answered.

I gave Mayee the keys and told her to go on ahead with the girls while I spoke to Kiki. She took the keys and walked off.

"Kevin, please tell me you didn't kill that man?"

"I didn't kill Nathan Kiki."

"Mommy is freaking out over this at the house."

"I can imagine."

"Kevin, I love you so much. Kurt's not here. It's you and me now. I don't have anybody besides you. Mommy's not going to be here forever. If I lose you I'll kill myself Kevin."

"Kiki don't ever say that shit again you hear me!"

Keisha started to cry on my shoulder. I hugged her close and told her to man up. She began to laugh as we walked towards the entrance. Before we got to my door, I asked Kiki what was going on with the girls. She told me they were worried about

Mayee. Cause they knew she was at my place. Me and Kiki finally reached my door. I rang the bell. Mayee opened the door. She had already put on her sweats and gotten comfortable on the couch with the girls. I could see by the look on their faces, that she had told them that she was pregnant.

"What are you all smiling at?" Kiki asked, smiling back.

"Kiki's going to be an Auntie!" Patricia said laughing.

"What?!" Kiki said holding her mouth.

"Congratulations Kevin!" Theresa said out loud.

"You know me Kevin. Oh shit! Oh shit!" Monica said jumping up and down.

"I love you Kevin." Mayee said with a serious expression.

"I thought you wasn't sure Mayee?" I answered, as I sat down beside her.

"I took the test three days ago. I wanted you to enjoy the test results for yourself."

"You chicks play too many games."

Everyone started shouting at me.

"Sit your punk ass back!" Kiki said.

"Nigga please!" Monica replied.

"You know what? That's why we don't tell you brother's shit!" Patricia screamed.

"Y'all better back off my baby daddy!"

Mayee said standing up waving her hands and snapping her fingers.

Everything seems to be back to normal. Even after what time may bring into one's life. I shook my head as I walked away laughing heading towards my room. I took my coat off and sat back on my bed. I pulled the box from under my bed and stared at it for a few seconds.

"Mayee, could you come here for a minute!"

I yelled staring at the box. She came running inside the room looking worried. Then she saw the shoebox sitting between my legs.

"No honey, you go ahead and read that to yourself. That's for you to read."

"But Jay said we should read it together."

She pushed me forward as she positioned herself behind me on the bed wrapping her legs around my waist. I opened the box and took out the envelope. It had nothing written on the front. Just a plain white envelope sealed shut. I opened the envelope and began pulling out what appeared to be an old used and worn out letter. I unfolded it and we stared at the date.

September 5, 1995

Dear Kevin Dawson:

I can't believe 1992 has come and gone so fast. I saw you the other day on 42nd Street having fun with your boy Kurt. I was taking my little brother Jay around 42nd Street to show him how beautiful New York City can be at night. You know, the pretty lights and the tall buildings.

I remembered the day you were telling me how you would come down to Times Square at night by yourself when you wanted to get away from all your problems. You also said if I ever wanted to feel something wonderful, even though it might seem like chaos was all around, all I had to do was stand still. You told me to open my arms wide, and look up at the tallest building where I could see the sunrise peeking over the horizon. And nothing else would seem to matter.

Today, my problems are weighing heavy around my neck. I'm in a relationship with this guy who's going to Law school, but this relationship is not a healthy one. And I'm going to break it off with him. But Today I took Jay down to 42nd Street. It's a lot different now, but Jay reminded me about what you said to him one day. It's amazing how a child can remember the smallest things. He remembers you more than I want him to at times. I'm not saying that in a bad sense Kevin. It's just hard to imagine why I didn't make love to you when I had the chance. I can't believe I just said that (smile).

Anyway, my brother says he misses you very much. All day he runs to every corner he sees, opens his arms wide and screams, "I can see the sunrise! I can see the sunrise!"

People look at us like we are crazy. But he doesn't care. I guess it's his way of escaping our current situation. I promised him if we ever were to see you again that he could give you this letter. He is excited at this very moment. We are at the park on 42nd & 6th Avenue right now. We come here a lot. He still looks for you.

Well Kevin Dawson, I know the chances are very slim that this letter will ever reach you. But for Jay to see the sunrise, I'll bring him here as long as it takes for him to be happy. I haven't seen the sunrise for a couple of years now. Do you still see the sunrise?

Love,

Sharon and Jay

P.S.   I'm still waiting for the sun to rise.

Coming Soon

By

Geoffrey McClanahan

The Epic Psychological Thriller Trilogy Collection

Parts 1, 2 & 3

The Chronicles of

"CRUSH ONYX"

"CRUSH ONYX2" ...Onyx Unleashed...

"CRUSH ONYX3" ...There can only be one...

Synopsis

Chronicles of

Crush Onyx

Author: Geoffrey McClanahan brings you a Psychological thriller that will shake the very fabrics of the Urban Writer's world. Theory of Psychoanalysis: Psychoanalytic theory has fundamentally changed the traditional conceptions of the manner in which the human mind functions and the role it plays in human life by manipulating instinctual drives. The Unconscious Mind; The part of the mind which gives rise to a collection of mental phenomena that manifest in a person's mind but which the person is not aware of at the time of the occurrence. The first of Sigmund Freud's innovations was his recognition of psychic processes. Take a journey into the psyche. Learn what it's like to live within the mind of Ms. Crush Onyx.

Crush finds out, in a horrifying betrayal, that after 35 years of experimental practices under the care of family physician Dr. Kenneth Korvach, she was born with a split personality. Her mind and worlds are split in half! The life she thought was her own is now shared between two! Crush; A reserved, wealthy, educated business Beauty and Onyx; A ruthless, sinister, serial killer who birthed two maniac twin offspring, Asteria and Leto without "Crush" even knowing. These deadly teenage killing beauties trained by the best serial killers from an underground cult (The Sandbox) lead by their mother "Onyx", obey her every command! Kill, Kill, Kill!

F.B.I. Agent Candice Sums is obsessed in her pursuit to capture Crush Onyx along with her 12 year partner and childhood friend Agent Michelle Blake. Dr. Kenneth Korvach beat the judicial system to release "Crush" on all murder charges due to her mental disorder by separating and repressing her alter ego personality "Onyx". Although they were taken off the case, they will stop at nothing until "Onyx" is locked away for good regardless if "Crush" is unaware that she was born mentally attached to "Onyx". Both agents continue to be turned inside out, discovering new horrors around every corner turned and through every door opened.

EliteRoyalties LLC Publications

www.ingramcontent.com/pod-product-compliance
Lightning Source LLC
Chambersburg PA
CBHW031338170626
46807CB00002B/751